First published by Armou

Visit http://deanclaytone

ISBN: 9781521153130

9 8 7 6 5 4 3 2 1

Copyright 2017 Dean Clayton Edwards

The right of Dean Clayton Edwards to be identified as the author of this work has been asserted by him in accordance with the Copyright, Designs and Patents Act 1988.

All rights reserved. No part of this publication may be reproduced, stored in or introduced into a retrieval system, or transmitted, in any form, or by any means (electronic, mechanical, photocopying, recording or otherwise) without the prior written permission of the publisher. Any person who does any unauthorised act in relation to this publication may be liable to criminal prosecution and civil claims for damages.

FRIDAY NIGHT

"There's a chair that wants to kill me. It was across the street when I looked out of the window last night and it was there this morning. Waiting. The obvious explanation, the one that gets you killed if you start to believe it, is that someone pulled it out of the new skip opposite my flat and decided they didn't like it after all. Maybe they started thinking about who had died in it. Or maybe it was broken - I'd not got close enough to see. Perhaps it was just ugly.

"Nobody pulled it out of the skip. It climbed out. By itself. I know how that sounds, but fortunately nobody is reading this and nobody ever will. This is just to keep a record of events and to help me rationalise. I know what is up and I know what is down and I know the sound of something throwing itself at the walls of a metal skip for three hours and twenty minutes until it manages to free itself.

"I didn't see it land and then right itself on the pavement, but I know it happened. The same way that I know it's looking longingly up at my living room window, even while I'm here at the office.

"It knows where I live and it knows I'm due home. It knows that I'll do almost anything to avoid it."

*

"What are you writing?"

I snapped my journal shut in response to the question. It made a dull, warm sound in the sterile office that was slowly emptying after an eight-hour day.

Hayley was on her way out of the building, with her

rucksack full of textbooks on her shoulder. Being the studious type, my furious note-making had caught her attention. She gave me a smile while she waited for my answer.

She had on a striped grey and black wool dress under a military style winter coat. Beneath her beret, her hair was tied back in a neat pony tail, and her eyes glistened; severe, blue eyes - clever and clear and cool.

While we still knew very little about each other, I made a lot of rapid fire decisions about our future together. I'd read that people end up with partners of roughly the same level of attractiveness, so I was punching above my weight.

"It's a journal," I said.

"Exciting day at the office?" she asked.

"Always."

"Must have been. You're normally first out of here in the evening."

"And last to arrive in the morning," I said. "I know. Lazy bastard."

"You convinced the management to create your own department, and then you ran it all by yourself, so you don't have to answer to anyone. It's genius, actually."

"Thank you. It really is also lazy."

"Wanna train me up?"

"There's barely enough work for one person," I said quietly.

"Don't sell yourself short. Things weren't the same here while you were away."

"I doubt anyone really noticed."

"I noticed," she said and while I was thinking about that, she added: "Anything about me in your journal?"

"I could tell you," I replied, "but then ..."

"... you'd have to kill me, right? Sounds like it would

almost be worth it." She came closer, but her eyes were on me, not on the book. "What's so exciting that you couldn't write that at home?"

"I'm in no hurry to get back," I said, thinking of the chair outside my flat and how it was facing my window, not hiding the fact that it wanted to get inside.

"Home's over-rated," she said, glancing at people packing up for the weekend. "But we can't stay here all night."

She started walking, her black leather boot heels thudding against the grey carpet tiles.

"Do you want to do something tonight?" I asked.

The words sort of spilled out like one long word. The guy sitting next to me dropped his pen.

My heart was hammering.

My philosophy at that point, more than ever, was that you need to do what scares you. You need to make a list of whatever is holding you back and confront those things one by one, crossing them off the list before they did the same to you.

If you're not paying close attention, your fears grow up around you, hatching out of wood, seeping out of the cracks, climbing out of skips. Before you know it they cast bigger shadows than you do. They take control of parts of you that you'd taken for granted. They develop capital letters and paralyse you so that you're Afraid to walk back to your flat after work. The emptiness you cultivated becomes the place they grow. They start to know you better than you know yourself.

Considering my beliefs on the subject of fear, I should really have been heading home to deal with the chair – to throw a cover over it, or douse it with petrol, or to saw its legs off, or something. But sometimes you have to work up to confronting your greatest fears. Taking smaller risks along the way can make you feel strong, especially when you manage to come out whole on the other side. Usually.

I thought all these things and more while her eyes remained fixed on mine and I wondered how much of me she really saw. I tried to keep my thoughts light while my body felt leaden and sweaty.

She wasn't smiling any more. She looked perplexed.

"... or we could do something next week?" I said, backtracking. So much for coming out unharmed.

"No," she said. "I was meant to be studying, but I can take a night off."

"You'd do that?" I said, frowning.

"Apart from more textbooks, I've got nothing waiting for me."

That could have been good or bad. If I'd had nothing but books waiting for me, I'd have been home already. For a moment, though, I was glad that the chair had settled outside my flat. If I hadn't been avoiding going home, I might not have had the courage to ask Hayley out.

The last group of office staff was filing out of the door, leaving Hayley, the guy at the next desk and me. The women said goodbye when they saw me looking and then they went back to their hushed conversation. They could see that something was still going on between me and Hayley and I was glad. I didn't care to know the content of their whispers though. They could go on thinking they knew everything about me that there was to know. It had worked for me for such a long time.

Hayley didn't appear to be aware of anyone else in the room. Her attention was focussed entirely on our conversation, not on what other people were thinking, and I envied her that.

"Shall we continue this outside?" Hayley said.

I slid my journal deep into the belly of my bag and then logged out of my machine.

"I've forgotten to log out," Hayley said thoughtfully, prompted by my activity.

The IT guys upstairs were doing another major upgrade of the network that evening, part of removing all the systems that didn't work well together and wiping the drives clean so they could start again with something better, something new.

Her desk was way on the other side of the office and I knew exactly where to look. On many occassions, I'd been aware of her footfall as she walked the long walk from her desk to the water cooler, from the water cooler to her desk.

"I also need to pee like a racehorse," she noted.

I laughed out loud, because I hadn't heard it put like that before.

"Could you log off for me?" she added, backing towards the door. "I'll meet you outside."

"Sure," I said. "No problem."

I said that on automatic, because it was the normal thing to say. I was good at hiding my anxiety. I poured it into my journal, so that I could keep smiling even when something like this was happening. All I wanted to do was follow her out of the room. I wanted to be the one waiting safely outside.

Continuing to smile, I was aware of uniform, blue fabric crowding my peripheral vision.

"See you out there," I agreed and she strode out of the room.

The Chair

That left me and the guy in the cubicle next to mine.

"I don't know how you managed that," he said with a grin. "She's so hot."

"Thanks," I said. "I think."

As the guy whose name I didn't even know put his bag over his shoulder, I finally looked across the office at the sea of chairs and almost doubled over in terror.

"Could you wait a minute?" I said to him, not knowing how I was going to explain that I couldn't possibly walk across this room just to log out of a computer. Not even for Hayley. She'd made such a simple, reasonable request, but there was no fucking way. There just wasn't.

"Got a train to catch," he said and he went towards the exit as quickly as I would have liked to.

The moment he left the room, I felt the familiar shift.

It was as if the awareness of every chair in the room, every unwatched chair in the building, turned towards me. They communicated silently with each other over distance. I don't know how, but I could feel their knowing. I could feel that they had been conversing about me.

I'd managed to avoid this happening in the office until now. I'd always imagined that this would be the worst possible place to be 'alone'.

On similar occassions, when I'd talked myself into standing alone in any furnished room, I reminded myself of the possibility that my fear was imagined. There was some comfort in the idea that I could be insane. Not completely mad. Functional, but with a piece missing, or a piece extra, depending on how you looked at it.

I kept my eyes on the floor. The shitty, grey tiles.

Any observer would have been quick to assure me that it was impossible to be harmed by office furniture.

They'd mean well. But I'd seen things that I couldn't explain and it was hard to ignore the evidence of my own eyes, no matter how much I wanted to believe that I was safe.

The room, conspicuously empty of human life now, was about half the size of a football field. Glaring striplights lit every corner and I was grateful for that. Still unable to look up for the time being, I listened out for anything approaching. All I heard was the hum of computers on standby. No doubt all of them had been successfully readied for upgrade apart from Hayley's.

Thinking of the IT team upstairs reassured me somewhat. Sure, I was alone in the room, but I wasn't alone in the building. Perhaps that would go in my favour.

The nagging voice in my head, however, reminded me that they were far enough from this floor that they wouldn't notice if anything untoward happened to me in here. They didn't answer their phones and were cited as saying that there was no such thing as an urgent email. At least two of them worked with headphones on. There could be a massacre down here and nobody would know until the next shift.

Increasingly nervous, I spied Hayley's desk in the distance. Reaching her computer would have meant walking the length of the office and there was no way I was going to do that by myself.

It doesn't matter if the thing you fear exists or not. Fear is real. Fear makes you forget to breathe and sticks your shirt to your neck, your chest, your back. It edges you towards the wall, while the dozen desk islands in the room seem to grow in stature, each one surrounded by groups of blue swivel chairs.

Most teams worked in groups of eight, which meant there were almost a hundred chairs in here and only one of me.

"She'll be back any second," I said out loud. "You know that."

The chairs didn't respond. They knew I was afraid and that was dangerous.

I threw my bag onto my shoulder and hurried through the exit without a look back.

*

I suggested a taxi, because I was exhilerated to have escaped the office unhurt and things like that made me want to spend money. Partly, though, I felt bad that I'd asked Hayley out and didn't have any wheels to back up the offer. It wouldn't have been like this a year ago. Then it would have been all about the wheels.

Every spare penny used to go on beer and doing up crap-looking cars for racing unsuspecting arseholes. I'd target people who didn't like to be left standing by a Skoda or a Datsun. I used to love the horrified looks on people's faces when I cut them up at the lights and left them for dead.

I don't think that would have impressed Hayley much though. Nor would failing to log off her computer. I was going to say something, but then it was actually raining. Grey clouds continued to gather above us, muscling out the last of the light.

"I don't mind getting wet," she said. "You?"

After that, I couldn't think about much else.

We let a black cab roll past us with its yellow 'taxi' light gleaming through the sparkling night. I was glad that we were walking. Crowds battling the worsening rain gave me an excuse to take her hand. Nobody was looking where they were going. Half of the blurred faces were masked by uniform black umbrellas. I navigated shoals of commuters across a busy intersection near Tower Bridge where I insisted on waiting for the traffic lights to change although people marched into the road around us and tutted at me for stopping. I, however, knew that drivers didn't stop their cars just because there were objects in front of them. Sometimes they sped up. Sometimes they were looking at their phones, or the rear view mirror, or they were arguing with their best friend about how women weren't the answer to their problems and looking at him with a raised eyebrow instead of noticing the bend in the road. Sometimes the road was wet and as the car swerved off the highway and over a pavement, it became pretty clear that they were driving too fast for the conditions, and then it was also clear - while spinning out of control - that it's too late to do anything about that and so they just instinctively loosen their grip on the wheel and smash through the barrier, writing off the car at that point, and continuing to bounce down the steep bank, towards a tree, with the brakes not seeming to have any effect at all.

I waited for the green man, squeezed Hayley's hand and led her across the road. She was evidently aware of my caution, because she said: "I heard you wrote your car off."

To her credit, she had at least waited until we were safely on the other side of the road before announcing that. Nonetheless, I tripped on cracked paving and my entire body spasmed with the shock of hearing her refer to my accident out loud.

"Was it bad?" she said. "I mean, were you hurt? You came back to work the week after. I wouldn't have known anything had happened except for a couple of people talking about it."

"Only a couple? What did they say?"

The Chair

"They said you were lucky to be alive. I don't speculate about that kind of thing myself. I think what they meant was, you could have died."

"The car was a mess," I said. "I was alright for the most part."

"You've been quiet since the accident," she said. "Not so much of a lad."

"Oh, really?"

"I have to admit, I like it. As long as you're okay, I mean."

I almost said that the accident was nothing to write home about, but I didn't want her thinking about my journal again. That was firmly for my eyes only. She'd think I was insane if she read that.

I tried to sound brave as I talked about lacerations and bruising, but I was lying about being hurt, because being pulled injury-free from a car that was crumpled like a cardboard box under a boot heel only makes a great story when you don't leave your best friend smashed against the dashboard and sort of pinned there like a bloody butterfly in a mad collection. My dying passenger ruined an otherwise good story.

I generally thought it best to avoid the details. I was loathe to tell it as it really happened. The accident was my fault. I'd been in the driving seat. I hadn't been watching the road. I'd been yelling at Charlie, who I now admit should never have been in the car. That was my fault too.

The accident was journal material only. Like the chairs. Nobody needed to know that stuff or how I felt about it. Except for Charlie perhaps, but I was working up to talking to him again. He'd survived the crash, no thanks to me. I didn't know if he'd want to hear from me, and I was afraid to find out.

Charlie and the chairs. Even though I avoided them, I knew they were out there. Monsters I'd created when I took my eyes off the road.

*

I held the door for Hayley and she strolled into the cinema without a word, like we'd been coming here every weekend for months already. In fact, this was only the third time we'd been outside of work together, including the Christmas party and a wine-tasting event where we'd both done too much tasting; I'd offered to walk her home and then I'd fallen asleep in the supermarket toilet.

It wasn't a glorious track record, but she seemed willing to give me another chance. Especially now that I was so 'quiet' after the accident. At least something good had come from the mental trauma of that car crash.

This was the first time we'd been alone together without people gawking. Perhaps our familiarity was the reason for feeling that words weren't necessary between us. I wished that all relationships could be nurtutered, maintained and repaired without words.

She took my arm. If felt natural. We laughed easily about movie posters, and about popcorn, about discarding the day to day bullshit our lives had become. Neither of us talked about the office. The cooler, the emails, the phonecalls, the machines whirring in front of empty chairs – they all seemed very far away.

We definitely didn't talk about car crashes anymore. We'd closed that book for the night.

We didn't discuss who was going to pay or, when the time came, where we preferred to sit. Spending time with her

The Chair

was as good as being by myself, only without the emptiness. And without the simmering sense of dread beneath every action.

I don't know why we fit so well into each other's puzzles, but we didn't let each other go the whole time we were together, except when we removed our coats to get more comfortable. We held onto each other like established lovers, but as if coincidence could separate us as easily as it had brought us to together.

I have to admit that I felt guilty about giving Charlie such a hard time about marrying Jeanette. We'd been mates for years and he'd never had a serious girlfiend, but then he got married and he started talking about having kids and we were too young for that kind of thing. Basically, she'd fucked him and then she'd fucked him up. I was in the process of telling him so, at my most eloquent, when I destroyed his life by spinning off the road.

Now, here I was, fucking hypocrite, going from 0-60 with Hayley.

There was a tightness to her grip on my arm that belied her cool exterior. And I'd responded by squeezing her forearm.

Feeling a sudden ache that I hadn't expected – maybe not love, but something real – I almost said:

"Are you fucking with me?"

But I decided to go with it and enjoy the moment instead.

We moved along the row at the very back of the cinema, which worked for me because having all the chairs in the room within sight was more important than being able to see the screen. There was nothing behind us but a wall and emergency exits on either side.

Like many cinemas, this one had started its life as a theatre for the stage. Little remained of the original building or its fixtures aside from its location next to the church beside Tower Bridge. I remembered the 'for sale' sign going up in front of the old place, and then the heavy, black graffiti, claiming the building before it was sold. The new owners didn't get rid of the graffiti. They just put a new sign over the tags and swear words. It was going to be a cinema. A few weeks later, demolition started.

Workmen in hard hats ripped fixtures from their moorings, destroying windows and walls, floors and foundations. They discarded sculpted flowers and busts, vases, paintings on threadbare canvas and beautiful bits of pillar. They dumped it all in skips amid plaster, rubble and glass. The theatre became a modern ruin.

A whole mound of seats grew outside the gutted building, many of the legs still attached. I started taking another route home, but sometimes, curious, I'd approach the site from across the road to see if the seats were still there. Some of them were stacked in towers, like monuments. Most were just piled on top of each other any old how, in an orgy of velour and steel. The whole lot shifted and creaked. The ground was littered with the bolts that had once fixed the seats in place.

On the day the pile disappeared, I stood across the street, looking over my shoulders, not quite able to breathe. I imagined the seats dispersing like spiderlings through the city streets, but I refused to run. You don't want to get into a spiral with fear. It took over an hour, but I made myself enter the worksite and I forced myself to walk this way home every evening after work as an act of defiance.

As the new building went up, I quickly saw that it

The Chair

was just like all the other cinemas in the chain. Every corridor would be well-lit. There would be CCTV cameras on the walls. It was going to be safe, even for me, despite what I knew was waiting in every single screen room.

I felt like this cinema was mine. I'd faced my phobia here and survived. Every time I went in, it was an achievement. Perhaps never more so than tonight.

While the adverts and then trailers rolled, I enjoyed the feel of Hayley's long fingers resting gently in my hand, her cool palm warmed by mine, and I let my eyes drift luxuriously over the familiar setting.

There was something disappointing and yet reassuring about the non-descript decor; the freshly painted walls and glowing spotlights. There were rooms like this all over London, all over the UK, all over the world, and not one of them contained something that could hurt me. Nothing bad had ever happened to me in a cinema, despite the sheer numbers of seats.

Here, the chairs were covered in a blue synthetic fabric, with those seats that you pull down and that spring back up when you stand.

Every seat was bolted to the ground and attached to its neighbour.

To the right of the dark room was the 'reserved' section for large groups like classes of film students or for when filmmakers attended their movie premieres. Those chairs were red and that bothered me, but I reminded myself that they too were fixed to the floor. Like the others, they faced the screen in their silent regiment.

Hayley handed me the popcorn while she shrugged off her coat and crossed her legs, which took my mind off everything but her until the lights dimmed and an image flickered to life on the screen.

Even then, I was still acutely aware of her proximity to me. Not just her body, and the feel of her arm on the armrest, and her smell – soap, no perfume – but her presence. I felt more solid, being a part of her evening. It was like taking a night off from being inside my head. I wondered if my presence was doing anything for her and she answered with a smile, illuminated by the garish cinema screen.

We made fun of the messages for fizzy drinks, fragrances and cars, making suggestions as to who the advertisers thought we were and what they thought we needed, who they thought we needed to be. We vowed to buy one each of all the products mentioned as soon as we left the cinema in order to solve all our problems.

"Fuck, it's so simple," she said.

I wanted to ask her about her problems. I wanted to hear all about them, but this wasn't the time or the place. Perhaps afterwards.

I was feeling special when the spotlights dimmed and the film started. The curtains opened a bit wider, revealing more screen, and some of the lights went out completely.

We weren't long into the movie before Hayley laughed at something and I took that as a natural opportunity to put my hand on her knee. I kept it there and it felt like an unknown appendage, like something I could lose if I wasn't careful, until she rested her head on my shoulder, her black hair tickling the skin of my cheek. That was when I knew that she would come home with me if I asked her. That was when I knew that I would invite her. That was when I saw something scuttle in front of the screen.

I leaned forward suddenly, choking on popcorn I'd been toying with in my mouth. My hand squeezed Hayley's thigh so hard that she yelped and people turned in their chairs to glare at us.

"Shhh!" they said.

"Steady," Hayley hissed. "I'm planning to use this leg later."

The running object - why skirt around it, it was a fucking cinema seat! - went from right to left. I searched the shadows for light glinting off some part of its metallic frame. Staring into the darkness, I knew that it would be able to hide in low light like this as long as it kept still. They were masters of patience. They crept. They shunted. They rolled an inch at a time and then waited for hours if necessary until they could move again. They almost never let you see them move; they started on one side of a room and when you turned your back, which I no longer did, they crept to the other. The cinema chair had wanted me to see it. If my date in the cinema was a power play, the chair had trumped me with a masterful stroke.

Body rigid, I searched the rows with my eyes, in a panic at first, but then systematically. Right to left. Next row. Left to right. All the way from row A to row U, where we sat.

The chair's movement had been silent, or rather its run had been masked by the rumbling soundtrack of the movie, so there was no way to prevent it sneaking up on me now but to keep turning left and right, like I was watching a tennis match.

I chewed at my lip, not only anxious and afraid, but confused. Every chair in here was meant to be bolted to the ground and attached to at least one neighbour. That fact, which now seemed more like a theory, was one of the key things that had always prevented me losing my shit in here. The other was that chairs had never moved before when other people were present.

It had to be said that nobody else seemed to be reacting as though they'd seen something incredible moving at the front of the room. Their necks were tilted back, staring up at the images.

I pretended to relax, for Hayley's sake, but while scanning the room, I saw it again. The chair was silhouetted briefly as it juddered along on two legs between the aisles and dove into the shadows between two rows of comrades. There was no doubt in my mind that it wanted me to see it. I'd got too comfortable.

"Up here," Hayley said and she adjusted my hand so that it was high on her thigh.

I was expecting her to ask me what was wrong, but it must have been too dark for her to see the expression on my face. Gently, she started to stroke my crotch, her eyes on mine.

"You weren't watching the film, were you?" she breathed.

"No," I admitted. "No, I wasn't."

"Me neither." She turned her body towards me, her knee jabbing into my thigh, and then started to undo my fly.

"Hayley. I ..."

"Shh."

She lowered her head and took me into her mouth.

The screen kept flickering, tricking me into thinking that the chairs around us were shifting. Or masking those that were really moving.

I was almost sure that nothing would happen as long as I was with Hayley, but then I'd been sure that they wouldn't move while the cinema was occupied and I'd been dead wrong about that.

"Hayley. Listen."

The Chair

"Relax," she said from my lap and continued sucking, teasing, pulling. Her mouth was warm. My balls must have been like ice.

I'd wanted this. This and more.

"Hayley!" I grabbed her and lifted her from my lap, at which point she gave up, sitting back in her chair with a thud and staring at the screen but not seeing it at all.

"What's up with you?" she hissed.

"I'm sorry," I said. I tried to make out the expression on her face. I think she was angry. I checked the aisles. Back to her.

She was forcing her way past me, spilling the popcorn all over the floor, hurrying out of the cinema with her coat in her arms.

"Hayley, wait!"

"Enjoy the film," she said.

I followed her out of the empty rowm but at the glowing exit, I glanced back at the room. I didn't see anything untoward, just a few people looking back over their shoulders to see what the fuss was about. I thought I heard laughter. It could have come from any of the moviegoers, but I knew that it hadn't. I rushed out of the imposing darkness and into the light, my world tilting.

*

"If I could take that back," I said, "I would."

"No more than I would," she said. She burst out of the cinema doors and into the courtyard, heading immediately towards the bridge.

"You took me by surprise, that's all," I said. "It wasn't your fault. It was all me."

"You don't have to explain," she said, throwing on her

coat and hauling her bag onto her shoulder. "Goodnight, Alan. Let's just pretend this didn't happen, okay?"

"This is the first time I've been myself with anyone since my accident." Yes. I used my accident to score points, but I meant it. "I don't want to go back to pretending."

"I'd much rather forget about tonight."

"Can we forget about it over a drink?" I said. "We could walk to my flat from here."

She laughed at that momentarily and I knew that I had her.

We stood there in the rain - her with her arms folded; me with my mouth open, wishing I knew what else to say now that I had her attention.

"I'm sorry," I said. "I thought there was someone watching us."

"It's a cinema," she said. "Nobody's there to watch us."

"Let me make it up to you. Let's go back to mine, put on a DVD and then not watch it."

Perhaps, like me, she was weighing up my offer against the likelihood of an agonising walk to her bus stop, during which I would not stop asking her to change her mind. Persistent fucker, me, and not enamoured with the idea of going home alone.

Hayley's dark eyes seemed hard and glassy. Perhaps she was already past my demands for her to change her mind and was already on the bus, using her card and then heading upstairs to sit at the back with the naughty kids and not look back at me at all.

She hadn't got as far as thinking about me walking home by myself, but I had. My brain was all over that one, sending pulses up and down my spine, making my hair stand

The Chair

on end and my knees give. I thought of the chair beside the skip, with its bottom lip all ragged from being eaten by mice. I imagined the chair shuffling underneath its shroud of cloudy plastic, making a sound like a rat in a nest of carrier bags.

The thought of the chair screwed me up like a piece of paper and let me tumble to the floor.

Perhaps it wouldn't stop with stretching, shifting and waiting. Perhaps it was ready to make its move on me tonight, as the chair in the cinema had evidently been. Perhaps all chairs would be bolder now.

I didn't want to face the armchair alone tonight after seeing its animate brethren in the cinema. What I'd seen only increased the chance that the armchair would blunder its way across the street to cut off my path. Even if I made it inside ... imagine waking to the sound of something pounding at the glass door with its own body.

"You don't get away that easily," I joked.

I extended my hand, gentle, but like I wouldn't take no for an answer.

*

Our hips bumped as we walked. As we approached my flat, which was only fifteen minutes on the other side of the bridge, I realised that I was just as pleased to be spending the evening with her as I was that I had someone to watch my back as I let myself into the flat tonight. I would have thought that the latter sensation of relief would have far outweighed the excitement of being on a date, but it wasn't so.

The armchair was still beside the skip. Puddles would have formed among the ridges and troughs of the plastic sheet. I wondered about that plastic sheet. Had the chair come from some place that was being decorated? Or had someone simply hated the sight of it? Maybe the plastic was a barrier between the chair and the world it affronted.

"Are you okay?" asked Hayley. "You seem tense again."

Aware of the chair watching us from beneath its plastic veil, I made extra efforts not to fumble my key fob, run inside or trip over my feet. I'd done all of those things the night before. I gave Hayley a squeeze and refused the chair a second glance. Fucking cunting thing. I put it out of my mind.

As much as possible.

*

Having followed me up the stairs to the second floor, Hayley stared at the comatose lift at the end of the hall. The light was on above it and I assured her that if you pushed the 'call lift' button, the arrow lit up, but the lift never arrived; we hadn't just climbed two sets of stairs for no reason.

The lift had been out of service for months and I was grateful for that, because it meant that nothing on wheels or wooden or plastic legs could get up here. There was no way a chair could get up stairs and use a door handle. In addition, the door to the corridor was one of those ones on a spring - it needed a fair amount of pressure to get it open and then it would shut firmly by itself afterwards.

Every evening I looked at the broken lift and entered the flat with a smile.

"That's more exercise than I've had in weeks," Hayley said, massaging her thighs as she entered.

"That's why I'm in such great physical condition," I said.

I noticed the dull thump of her boot heels on my IKEA rug, which I had to admit looked more and more like a

The Chair

dead cow, but at the time I'd simply wanted things to be black and white and soft.

Perhaps the glass coffee table could have done with a mug or a crumb-laden plate. This was all too much like a show home. It didn't look like someone lived here, and she'd be right if that was what she was thinking. I didn't so much live here as hide.

Her boot heels studded the bare boards. So sexy. She glaced into the bedroom, where you could sort of see my bed, too neatly-made, and movie posters on the walls where the car posters had been: Pulp Fiction above the bed with Mia Wallace gazing out of her world into ours, and the edge of Suspiria. From her angle, she probably couldn't see the beautiful woman dancing and dripping with blood. I hadn't really thought much about the effect the poster might have on female visitors; the stark black, white and red had matched my colour theme and I thought it was a cool movie. I hadn't really thought about this place as a shag pad, evidently.

I had poster for Vertigo for the same aesthetic reasons, with a silhouette of James Stewart spinning down into a hole. I wished I'd stopped with that.

There were more potted plants in there though, flowering. At least something in this flat had been flourishing.

Hayley peeked through the open door on the other side of the flat to the kitchen. Small. Functional. Everything in its place.

"Most guys live like pigs." she said. "Do you really live alone?"

"I couldn't live any more alone than this," I said.

"I know what you mean."

She surveyed my bookshelves and I mentally riffled through my book collection ahead of her, wishing I had more exciting reading tastes. though I didn't know quite what that might entail.

There were a load of books about cars and racing up there that were no longer relevant to my life at all, mostly gifts from people who had known me as I was a year ago, before the accident, confident, optimistic, whole.

She picked up the one remaining Get Well Soon card. It was from my mum. I'd torn the others up and thrown them away as soon as they came out of their envelopes, but that one I'd kept, long enough for it to send a shower of dust into the air when Hayley blew on it. I'd kept it partly because it had a picture of a sports car on it, and I thought it was funny that my mum didn't get the irony of that or maybe she did and she was just rubbing it in. I'd thrown out my model cars, even the Ferrari F40 and the Trans Am like the car out of Knight Rider. I'd torn a poster of a Porsche off the back of the wall. It was like I'd grown up overnight, grown up into nothing. I made empty spaces and did nothing to fill them. Anything to do with fast cars, crashing them and almost killing friends had to go.

Someone was leaving their banger in my designated parking space round the back of the building. People in this building had been crucified on the public announcement board for less, but my once fiercely-guarded parking space didn't matter to me anymore. I couldn't imagine driving through the streets of London again for a good long time.

Mum had known that I hadn't been injured, but she'd given me the card anyway.

I didn't feel that I could put that card away until I was feeling well. Physically I was fine; other parts of me had been damaged. My ego, my future, my optimism: those things had cracked. Mum thought she knew how I could fix them.

The Chair

"It says 'Talk to him'," read Hayley, waving the card around like she needed to do that to illustrate a point. "Is this about the accident? Who's 'him'?"

"Charlie," I said, a chill passing through me and threatening to carry me away.

She's going to make me phone him, I thought. If I don't get that card out of her hand, she's going to realise that Charlie was my passenger and that I haven't talked to him since the accident and then she'll think I'm a monster and she'll tell me that I need to go and see him. Any part of that was enough to ruin this evening.

"Sometimes you need to face your fears head on," she said. "They're probably not as bad as you think."

I wondered if she'd somehow snuck a peak at my journal and I glanced at my bag, next to hers on the floor. It was all done up, like it was supposed to be.

"Don't let it consume you," she said, probing. "Don't wait until it's too late. I could help."

Suddenly, I had a thought, a flicker of memory. "What are you studying?" I asked.

"Psychology," she said.

It hadn't seemed important before the accident, but now it brought me out in a cold sweat.

"PTSD this term," she admitted.

Oh shit.

"Do you think I'd make a good case study?" I heard myself say.

Stop talking, I told myself.

"Is there something you want to tell me?" she asked, adding with a smile: "Lover-Patient confidentiality."

Looking at her form, like something cut from the office and pasted into my flat with the edges unfeathered, solid and real in a flat that had become almost ethereal to me over the months, like in a dream where nothing happens but there's a door that might open and the worst thing in the world might come out, I realised that I wanted to protect her, from anything and everything. From me.

I'd already established in my mind that I was not like other guys. I was borderline nuts. I knew that. But she wasn't like other women either or at least I didn't feel about her the way I felt about anyone else I'd dated. For a start, I'd asked her to come into the flat. That was a first.

I felt like I could be vulnerable with her, which was reassuring, but that I wasn't vulnerable at all, which was unexpected and exciting. I felt like I could do anything, as long as she was watching.

I promised myself that if tonight went well, I'd phone him. No, I'd text him. No, I'd phone him. Then see him. If it let me have her, even if only for a few months, I'd do anything the universe demanded.

"What are you thinking?" she asked.

"Come here," I said.

She turned her smiling face up at me, deliberately tight-lipped. A last act of resistance since our failed adventure in the back row of the cinema.

I pressed my lips to hers, wondering what I would do and how ridiculous this might be if she didn't open her mouth in return, but she did, and soon it was unclear who was kissing who. The flat disappeared, spiralling down the same hole as James Stewart. Hayley was Mia Wallace, open, making me the best version of me I'd ever been, when really maybe I should have just said goodnight, jerked off and gone to bed, alone.

I was the dancer in the dark, oblivious to the blood.

The Chair

SATURDAY MORNING

I didn't need to look around to know that she was no longer in the flat. The sheets were cold and so was I.

There was no message from her on my phone, on the glass coffee table nor in the kitchen. There was no sign that she had been here at all, except for her smell on the bedsheets and pillow. The scent was primarily soapy, like that of a cheap shampoo, but it made my heart beat faster all the same. It was part of her smell and I allowed it to fill my nostrils, to fill me up entirely so that I could face the day from a position of strength for once.

On opening the blinds, the light made the flat seem brighter, a space with potential to be enjoyed, not survived. I felt I'd been brought up to speed with the changes that had been going on around me, like I'd been given yet another second chance.

I sighed, because I knew there was something awful I had to do to pay for this luck.

My phone battery was fully charged and I was out of excuses.

Before I could allow myself to think about it, I scrolled through the names on my phone until I got to CHARLIE, hit 'call' and climbed back into bed. Deep into bed. Traditionally, nothing can hurt you when you're under the covers. I closed my eyes to disappear into the darkness.

To my dismay and complete surprise, he picked up.

"Charlie?" I shat.

A woman answered. Jeanette, with a voice that would cut an open plan office in two. She'd always struck me as being headmistress-like. She used to peer at me over her glasses, which made me think of them as spectacles and I resented her causing the word 'spectacles' to pop up in my ordinary usage. I resented her for marrying my best friend and gradually castrating him in front of me. I resented her for being right every time she complained that I was a bad influence on him.

Even when things had been good between Jeanette and me, things had been shit, but they had been a fuck of a lot better then than they were now.

"Why are you calling here?" Jeanette asked.

I didn't tell her that was a really fucking strange question. I was so deeply in the wrong that I couldn't afford to be anything but on my best behaviour. I had to be perfect from now on, which was difficult because I still couldn't face the truth.

"I called to talk to Charlie," I said, like I hadn't almost killed him.

She responded by not responding.

My heart was hammering away inside me and sending blood to beat at my ear drums.

"Is Charlie there?"

Her breathing.

The Chair

"Don't hang up," I said.

Funny. We'd gone from 'coming of age movie' to 'psychological thriller', but it was as if we were reading from the same script as always.

"I wanted to talk to Charlie, because I have to tell him that I'm sorry. I'm sorry for everything. I wanted to come and visit after the accident, but, you know, you threw me out and I thought I'd give you some space and then a couple of days, became a week, which became a month, and then I just couldn't face him. And then when I felt I could face him, something happened to me. I don't really want to get into it on the phone and it's probably nothing compared to what Charlie's going through, but something happened to me. Maybe something got shaken loose in the accident, but I started ... things started ... I thought that I was ... and that things were ... let's say that things went a bit crazy and maybe I did too ... except ... Jeanette?"

There was no response.

"Are you there?"

I don't know at what point the line had gone dead.

My hand was shaking so much that the phone spilled from my fingers. My entire body trembled.

"That went badly," I said to myself. I thought that saying it out loud might make it better than it was, less globally and cosmically awful.

The best thing about the call was that Jeanette had hung up before I'd done any more irreparable damage.

Sweating under the covers, I pretended that I was in a decadent family grave. I'd been forgotten, blissfully non-existent in every realm.

Inhaling Hayley's scent on my pillow, I imagined she was with me, giving me a mock punch on the arm, a finger across my cheek, an arm around my waist, telling me to try again, because I could do anything.

The last thing I'd said to Charlie while he had been conscious was that a woman could never be the answer to his problems, certainly not Jeanette.

It was a good thing he wasn't here to see me now, sniffing the soap smell on Hayley's pillow for the strength to move.

Neither Jeanette nor Hayley answered their phones.

*

To get to the back of the furniture store, I had to pass an entire section of sofas and armchairs, leather, cotton, reclining, corner. I occupied the public space with them in a complicit silence - them knowing that I was aware of their sentience; me knowing that if they moved, there would be witnesses.

I counted four or five other customers in the store, in addition to two women in casual clothes serving and two guys in blue overalls arguing over some boxes at the back of the store. It was the two guys in overalls that I was interested in. I'd seen them a couple of times, and they'd definitely seen me, while attempting to desensitize myself to my fear of chairs. I'd had to avoid those guys' curious' glances and ignore their sniggers, but now I'd come explicitly to ask for their help.

As usual, the furniture at the rear of the shop was untidy, much of it in the process of being unpacked and cleaned up. Some of it was still wrapped up in packaging paper or plastic coverings, like the dreaded armchair opposite my flat.

I walked among a small, black, leather swivel chair

The Chair

that looked like a miniature version of every black, leather swivel chair I'd ever seen, a modern, red monstrosity like a sore tongue on stilts and a wide, wooden deck-chair type thing with furry pads attached to make a seat and a seat back, but which looked like it had killed a dog in the process of unfolding itself. I felt an unpleasant spark of electricity between us.

"I see you," I said, asserting my authority, choking down my fear.

They pretended not to react, but I could feel them clenching up. Without obviously moving, they seemed to prepare themselves, like snakes about to strike.

"Don't do anything stupid," I said, hands on hips. "There are cameras everywhere."

Although my stomach was turning, I knew I wouldn't come to harm in here as long as somebody somewhere was watching or recording. That had been the problem in the cinema: the room had been occupied but everyone was fixated on the screen, not the thing crawling below it.

"Give me any shit," I said, "and I'll buy you and take you apart with a screwdriver."

An appreciable silence spilled from them as I enjoyed my advantage.

"How would one of you like to come back with me and play by my rules for a change? No, I didn't think so."

The thought that anything I bought would become the object of a rescue attempt - rescue and revenge - took the edge off my enjoyment of the moment. I imagined this strange brood showing up in the night and being thwarted by the stairs. Still, the idea of waking up to a foyer full of self-motivated chairs gave me pause and I regretted how bolshy I'd been. Overcoming your fears and poking them with a stick were not the same thing.

I continued on my way, resisting the urge to look over my shoulder to see if they were all facing me now.

The two guys in overalls carried a massive chest between them. The first guy was tall and skinny, with angular limbs like branches, while the other guy was short enough for the chest to be carried at a sharp angle. Although smaller, he seemed to be the stronger of the two. They muscled the trunk into the second-hand area and dropped it.

The first guy grimaced, revealing silver front teeth, and wiped sweat from his large forehead with a dusty sleeve. The other guy eyed me with bright blue eyes and held up a hand to warn me off.

"We don't work here," he said. "If you want to buy something you want to talk to one of them ladies up front."

"He's just browsing," the tall guy said, evidently having recognised me from one of my previous desensitisation attempts at the store. He was smirking. I wondered if he'd seen me doing anything embarrasing and how much he knew about my ... condition.

"Do we look like Waterstones?" the short guy said.

"Do you ever do private jobs?" I asked.

The tall guy shook his head and the short guy said: "Yes. Collections. Removals. Seven days a week."

"I don't need a removal," I said. "I need something moved in. It's a small job, an armchair, but I can't do it by myself."

The man in charge slapped his colleague on the arm.

"Get the diary, will you?" he said. "Let's see when we can fit fella in."

"I need you to move it in today," I said.

I could still smell Hayley on my T-shirt. I was

thrumming with her and still felt superhuman. If I waited until tomorrow morning, I'd change my mind.

"A chair?" the tall guy scoffed.

"I'll pay you for a full hour," I said.

"And mileage," the shorter guy said, peering at me.

"It's just down the road," I said.

"That's what they all say."

To have my life back, to have a chance at a normal relationship with Hayley, yes, I'd pay mileage.

*

At just before nine that evening, a white van pulled up directly beneath the flat. I threw on my coat before jogging down the stairs to meet the driver and passenger, intent on intercepting them before they could change their minds and drive away.

"It's over there," I said, since they hadn't seemed to have figured it out yet.

They looked at the skip and then back to me as if I were crazy.

"Not the skip," I said. "The chair. Next to it."

I hung back as the smaller guy, Geoff, lifted the plastic sheet, which was rustling in the breeze.

Under the skirt of decaying plastic, I saw its feet.

All this time, the thing had been poised gnarled feet that seemed to be rolled up on themselves, like the end of jesters' shoes. The legs themselves were large and squat, suggesting great power. The sight of them made me stop in the middle of the street. The bigger guy, Art, saved me from oncoming traffic.

I tried to keep in mind that someone had designed those feet and had carved them that way. I reminded myself that the chair had not been born, but made.

Some chairs seem to be standing, like the regiments of seats in the cinema, while others give the impression of being seated themselves. This chair was somewhere between the two. I had no idea if the legs had buckled under the weight of its body, or if it had been caught mid-spring and was now frozen like this until we looked away.

My eye flashed up one of those frozen legs and I saw that the artist had gone overboard with the decoration. It was like he was trying to hide something in a frenzy. The design was largely floral and leafy, but there was something hair-like about it all too. It was all across the bottom of the chair.

Someone had probably loved this chair once. It might have fit in somewhere with a chandelier and an oak dining table with doilies and placemats, original, pastoral scenes on the walls, net curtains over the windows. It would look ridiculous in my flat. It would look terrifying.

It wasn't too late to ask the guys not to carry this inside. They'd be relieved, especially if I paid them anyway.

"It's wet," said Geoff.

I imagined that it had soiled itself, excited by my proximity.

"It rained," I said. "Of course, it's wet."

"You still want it?" Geoff asked.

"Yes," I made myself say. "It'll dry."

The men assumed their positions and grabbed hold of the chair under the seat, one at the spine and one at the mouth end.

"You brought us out here for this?" Geoff muttered.

"I can't move it myself," I said.

"Yeah, but why would you want to? No offense, but it's a piece of shit, isn't it?"

The Chair

"Possibly antique shit," Art said.

I watched the chair for a reaction. There was none.

"It has to be this chair," I said quietly. "And it has to be now."

"Why?"

Because it's been taunting me, and this is the last thing it expects. Because I'm afraid of it and I don't want to be afraid anymore.

Because you can't let your fears consume you.

They lifted it, not waiting for a further response from me. A wise move.

When they set the chair down in the foyer, I advised them that the lift was out of order.

"You're fucking kidding me," Geoff said. "What floor you on?" He covered his eyes as if he had a migraine.

I told them I was three flights up.

"You're fucking joking me!"

He glared at me as he bent down to lift the chair again and his colleague took the other side. Their postures were all wrong, particularly bad since this was their profession, and I told them so.

"You want to shut your mouth, sunshine," grumbled Geoff and he wasn't wrong, but I glared right back at him, trying to feel in control of something, because this bastard chair was moving ever closer to my flat and soon it would be inside. My throat and chest would be so tight that I wouldn't be able to breathe at all and the chair wouldn't have to do anything but smile to extinguish the little bit of me that was left.

"You gone deaf?" Geoff said. "Get the door!"

I pushed the swing door open with my back, which put me as close to the chair as I'd been so far. It made me think about what would happen later, when they were gone and I was alone with it.

To avoid full-scale panic, I focused on the chair's likely materials – wood, gold leaf, leather, foam stuffing. It didn't seem to smell of anything, at least not with the plastic covering still taped on. The sheet rustled and made crackling sounds like distant thunder. The chair legs brushed mine horribly and then the men started up the stairs with it, with me open-mouthed, regretting everything, beneath.

"Being wet makes it heavier," Geoff's colleague said. He sounded almost cheerful, despite his evident subservience.

"I hope you're going to enjoy sitting in this piece of crap," Geoff told me. "Before it caves in on you, that is."

It sounded like a curse, the way he said it like that.

I was never going to sit on it.

I wasn't planning to turn my back on it.

The two guys crept up the stairs one step at a time, shifting their hands and shunting and grunting and sliding along the walls and tripping and falling and leaning on the creaking bannisters. I knew that the chair wasn't going to fall, because while barrelling into me would have pleased it, it wanted most of all to be inside my flat and it wouldn't do anything to jeapordise that. For all I knew, it was shifting its body in their hands to make their grips more comfortable. It was finally getting what it had wanted for days. People had stolen or salvaged other items from the skip, but the chair hadn't let anyone take it.

The closer we got to my floor, the more I realised that I was completely unprepared for this.

On the third floor, they half fell and half-threw the chair through the double doors, stumbling into the corridor. Geoff was red in the face.

The Chair

I thought that it would have been funny if the lift had gone ping at that moment and the doors had trundled open, but it didn't. Despite appearances, it was dead.

"Not far now," I said, drawing my key and showing them the way.

The chair's castors scraped against the tiles as though they weren't turning at all, filling the corridor with a grating sound, and scarring the floor. There was a heart-wrenching space where there should have been a sound of crumpling cardboard and tinkling glass.

"Could you lift it?" I asked.

"No," snapped Geoff.

The only time they lifted the chair, now that they were on my floor, was to get over the threshold and into my living room. I opened up my door and pushed it wide, so I wouldn't need to be near the chair as it went in. I'd practically be hiding behind the open door, using it like a shield.

For a moment, the chair looked like there could have been someone sitting in it, perhaps a Queen lifted on her throne. It got stuck briefly in the doorway, because it was too wide to go in without being angled. Geoff grunted and shoved until the two of them were able to get the beast inside, at which point they continued by rolling it across the room.

I wasnt too concerned about the scratches on my floor. I was imagining the chair's sharp angles and how they might dig into flesh. What the chair had done to the floor was nothing compared to what it might do to a human body. I was thinking about how deep a scratch had to be before it drew blood. Not that deep. We were all so vulnerable, all so close to the surface.

Geoff gave it a final shove with his knee and it skidded another foot into the middle of the room, where there was plenty of space beside the Ikea 'cowskin' rug and the glass coffee table. He looked around the room briefly and smirked, as if he were thinking of horrible things to say about my living space, but there was nothing he could have said that was worse than what he'd just done by dumping this chair here, at my request.

"Happy?" Geoff asked, his eyes laughing at me, and the question resounded deep inside me, like a penny cast into a well, not touching the sides, disturbing the still, shallow, silt water.

"There's one more thing I'd like you to do," I said, keeping my voice low the way people do when someone malicious could be listening in. "It's going to be my reading chair. I always fall asleep when I read in bed. Since you're here, do you think you could move it into ...?"

After a long stare, Geoff positioned himself behind the chair without a word, seeming genuinely affronted by my demand and a step closer to punching me. He rolled the chair across the floor, with more scraping of wheels against boards, and he slammed it into the door jam. To my relief, it was too wide to roll in through the bedroom doorway. The fit was even tighter than it had been getting it through the entrance to the flat. Despite manhandling it, the chair would not go in and so they had to lift and tilt it, no mean feat judging from their groans and gasps and the flourishing red of their faces.

"On its side, on its side, you nob!" barked Geoff.

"It is on its side!"

"More! On its side more!"

Geoff put his entire weight against the chair in an attempt to force it through the doorway, even if that meant sacrificing my door jamb, while the other guy ended up sort of trapped underneath it, trying to pry it free without losing a

The Chair

hand or having the chair crush him.

I had to look away while they worked. This was nightmarish.

"Angle it, angle it!" Geoff snapped. "The other way! Angle it the other way!"

They chipped chunks off the door jamb. Debris hit the floor and paint smudges scarred the chair's legs. The tall assistant trapped a finger and yowled, a sound that made Geoff snigger but caused me to stand very still, ice cold.

Wrinkled leather and greasy-looking wood thudded repeatedly against my painted, white door frame. I could hardly stand it.

Thud! Thud! Thud!

The plastic covering tore, like a mask being ripped off.

Thud! Thud!

I imagined the chair performing all these actions by itself, throwing itself at the doorway, snarling, shredding itself to get to me in the night.

Thud!

Geoff finally let the chair fall. His colleague jumped out of the way to avoid a broken toe. Geoff was exhausted and furious. His partner seemed genuinely disappointed that after all we had been through together the chair wouldn't fit where I wanted it. I didn't really want it in the bedroom, of course. Their failed attempt reassured me that the chair would not be able to enter my bedroom of its own accord, even if it managed to fumble my door open.

"Don't tell me you want it downstairs again," Geoff warned me.

"It can stay where it is," I said. I stared at the chair with my mouth hanging open, the way a child might stare at a darkened doorway.

When I heard their feet and coats shuffling, I waved a couple of notes in their direction. One of them snatched them from me - probably Geoff.

"We might as well have a good look at you after all that," said the assistant and he tugged at a corner of plastic.

"Leave it!" I yelled.

He gave me a curious look, like he'd only just realised that I might have a problem, before starting after his colleague.

I listened to them conferring in the hall, laughing, futily calling the lift, because they hadn't quite believed me when I said that it was broken. And then they were throwing open the double doors to plunge themselves into the stairwell.

In my living room, my former safe place, the chair was half disrobed.

I could see the shitty leather, so like skin that I felt bile rising in my throat. It was tanned, so tanned that it was burnt and cracked and I could see the meaty flesh beneath, white as mould. It seemed to have varicose veins in places and it was sort of oozing from an unknown source. I wondered if I would get home from work one evening and find that the chair had left a trail around the room, like a slug, as it explored my things.

There were things I could have said then, but the words wouldn't be spoken. It was like there wasn't room for them and me and it in the same room.

Its twisted feet and bent legs still made it look like it was either about to collapse or was readying itself to spring at me.

I took a very slow step back and it didn't twitch.

Already, I could feel it dominating the room.

The Chair

Dominating me.

Somehow, it fit. Those guys, me, Hayley: we were superimposed onto the landscape. This armchair, however, looked as though it had been here for 70 years, as if my minimalist aesthetic had taken shape around it. My sparse, modern decor shrinked as the chair absorbed all the oxygen - all the everything - in the room.

The seat looked really big indoors. Squatting there like that, I could imagine two children sitting on it quiet comfortably, not knowing, bouncing up an down, draping themselves over the arms, ignorant of the danger all around them.

Anxiously, I noted that while the chair had been too cumbersone to fit through the bedroom door, the delivery guys had deposited it exactly between me and that intended sanctuary. I'd have to walk within six feet of it to enter my room.

"It's just me and you now," I said and watched for some flicker of its dormant intelligence. A predator's patience, not its speed, was its greatest advantage.

I could feel the chair from across the room. I could feel its awareness.

Six feet was much closer to it that I wanted to be, but I could run it in a couple of seconds. The problem with running was that I didn't want the chair to know just how afraid it was making me feel. As much as I tried to control my heart rate and my breathing, it knew I was on edge and it was pleased, but I doubt it knew just how deep this dread went. Even I hadn't known until now.

I gave up on the bedroom. Instead, I forced myself to turn my back on the chair in a premature but much needed demonstration of power. I sauntered towards the kitchen, resisting every impulse demanding that I should turn around and not be a fool, just turn around and see if it was coming for me. I resisted, even though my hairs were on end and I could feel it watching me.

Walking as slowly as I could stand, I listened for the sound of castors half-rolling half-scraping over the boards.

I was almost into the kitchen when a hissing sound made me glance over my shoulder and I saw the last of the plastic sheet sliding to the boards like skin shuffled off by a snake.

The plastic could have slid off by itself, I told myself. The delivery guy had given it a good tug before I yelled at him, and it had almost come off when they'd tried to shove the chair through the bedroom door. It would have been perfectly normal for the plastic to fall to the floor on the suggestion of a breeze.

Logically, chairs couldn't move. I knew that. Chairs shouldn't have freedom of movement, nor the will to exert it. Logically, I shouldn't have had to do this. Logically, I shouldn't have been afraid.

Revealed in its entirety now, my eyes explored the ominous stains all over it. Not blood. That might come later, but the dirt of many backs and many bums, of shirts and suits, smoke and the street, insulting the pristine leather with grey and black. If you thought about it really hard, you could imagine that it had once looked good in a showroom or on the pages of a catalogue. It might even have been white, rather than having the tone of rotten egghshell. It would have been passable at least. Imagine that, and now imagine it in the present day. A nearly dead thing, dragged up the stairs to live out the end of its foul existence in my home.

Its arms were wood covered in leather, reminiscent of

The Chair

the wings of a muddy swan. Swans were notorious for breaking arms.

Forcing myself to look away again, I became acutely aware of my neck, my legs, my arms, all the vulnerable parts of me that a chair could pierce or shatter.

Safely inside the kitchen now, I flicked on the kettle. While it grumbled on the stand, I did my utmost not to keep peeking into the living room. I had the impression that the chair was moving almost imperceptibly, but I knew that fear could make people see things that weren't really there. I reminded myself that this chair was such a monster that if and when it moved there'd be no mistaking it. I comforted myself with that. The worst thing is that it worked.

As the boiling water made the kettle rumble in its electrified cradle, I stared at the chair again.

There were scars in the wood, indentations full of mud or mould.

One of the legs looked like someone had taken an axe to it and lost.

I reminded myself that I'd not yet been attacked by any chair, ever, anywhere. I'd seen one in full attack mode, but I personally had no scars or bruises or other evidence of a generalised malice. I had no physical proof that they could even move, only the evidence of my eyes and ears, which could have lied. I'd been under a lot of stress.

I told myself all this over the course of forty minutes, while I boiled and reboiled the kettle for a cup of tea that seemed so inappropriate and so impossibly sane. I was avoiding the inevitable. At some point, I would either have survived the weekend unscathed, in which case I'd know that I was insane because chairs definitively couldn't move, not even this one, that wanted me so badly, or I'd receive a physical injury, which, if it didn't kill me, would prove that I wasn't insane. In the event that I was attacked, I hoped that it was something that could be traced back to the chair, like a big bite or strangulation. Something I couldn't do to myself.

I wished that I wasn't doing this alone, but it was the only way. Insane or not, chairs only moved when it was me and them.

Besides, the only people I trusted enough to accompany me on this adventure were Charlie and Hayley and I didn't want either of them to see me in this condition. Especially not Hayley, who hadn't seen it before. I was wary of spending much more time with her until I was more straightened out, in one direction or another.

I don't know exactly when I realised that the chair was growling. It was the sound the largest guard dog you've ever seen might make on sensing an intruder. It seemed to emanate from deep within the chair. Shaken by the malicious rumble, I took it not as a warning but as an expression of its intense hatred for me and its great glee at being here to tell me face to face.

I could see the seat cushion moving up and down like a great top lip.

Removing the rubber door stopper allowed the kitchen door to swing shut so I didn't have to see the chair anymore and it could no longer see me.

The kettle rumbled on its stand and the switch clicked, leaving a tense and deliberate silence which I preserved by holding my breath, listening now for the chair's movements so I'd know whereabouts in the flat it was. I, on the other hand, was trapped. There was nowhere for me to go except into the living room or out of the window, in which case I'd have to drop down three storeys. I didn't fancy my chances of completing that escape without at least breaking an ankle. An injury like that would make me more vulnerable. Or worse, I could be incapicated to the extent that I ended up in a hospital bed, with an empty visitors' chair right next to me while I slept, all during the day, all during the night.

I kept looking at the window though, because right now the risks of jumping were preferable to opening the door to the living room.

"I need to arm myself," I said. "I need a weapon."

It wasn't like I'd never thought about what household items could be used as weapons in the event of an intruder getting in. I think all guys think about this kind of thing. I just wouldn't have thought I'd be using these items to tear into furniture.

Naturally, my hands went to the sharp knife in the wooden block beside the sink and the cook's blowtorch in the drawer. I'd hardly used either of them so the knife was sharp and the blowtorch felt full of gas. Thus armed, a box of matches on the counter, I stood at the closed door, psyching myself up to re-enter the living room.

The quiet was wrong. It was vibrating as though something was happening on the other side of the door. The sooner I opened the door, the sooner it would stop, but I couldn't quite bring myself to do more than turn the handle. Instead, I agonised over whether to open the door a crack and peer out, which ran the risk of having my fingers crushed, or to kick the door open, which would take the chair by surprise but would also mean that I'd be faced with whatever it was doing out there, all at once; an assault on my senses.

I lit the blowtorch and then gripped the knife in an overarm position.

At the door, I listened and counted to three.

Then I decided to take the edge off by counting to ten. Bursting out there with the blowtorch blazing would only make this fear worse.

As far from the door as possible, I slid down the wall to a sitting position on the floor.

All the while, silence seeped from the other room. That didn't necessarily mean that the chair wasn't animate. It meant that the chair was probably smarter than I'd thought.

Eventually, however, it ran out of patience, because I heard the sound of its castors against the wooden floor, like distant thunder rolling towards me.

"I told you!" I wanted to say, but there was nobody here but me and it, and it was time to go out there and face it.

The Chair

MONDAY NIGHT

"You weren't at work," Hayley said, her voice coming out of the mobile phone in my hand.

"No," I agreed sleepily, wondering what time it was.

"Thanks for logging me out," she said.

"... Ah." That seemed such a long time ago. "Yeah, about that … I …"

"What's going on with you? Are you okay?"

"Yes," I said, squinting against the glare of the neon striplight. It would seem so. The kitchen door was still closed. There were no visible dents in it; not on my side anyway.

"Why weren't you at work? Or is it a secret?"

It was Monday evening, which meant that I'd missed a day of work because I'd been trapped in my kitchen for three days.

"Something came up," I said, wiggling my feet to get the pins and needles out of my legs.

"Speaking of coming up, I'm outside."

I stumbled across the room to lean out of the window. Seeing her below, I dropped my key down.

I left the window wide open. I'd done what I could, washing my shit and piss down the sink and bleaching it, but you could still tell that I hadn't left this room for a long time and that nature had taken its course in a big way more than once.

A minute and a half later, Hayley let hersef into the flat.

I was poised at the kitchen door, timing it so that I emerged from the kitchen as she walked into the living room and I shut the door firmly behind me.

I suffered a panic about the carnage she would find, but that fear was nothing compared to the fear of leaving this room alone. There hadn't been a lot of noise over the weekend, but I'd heard enough to keep me in a circular debate with myself about how much food I had in the kitchen and whether or not it would be worth exiting from a window three storeys up. Shuffling sounds, like a pig snuffling through rubbish. Thudding against the walls at random times of the day and night, stopping as suddenly as it started. Those casters were like blunt knives tearing at my bare boards, slicing their way into my dreams.

I don't know what I'd been expecting to find when I entered the living room, but I was surprised by the lack of items out of place.

Three days I'd been in the kitchen. Three days and there was not so much as a scratch on the walls.

"Hi," Hayley said.

She was wearing a long black coat with the collar up and her hair down. Her presence in the room seemed to make sense of everything. Just like that, I wasn't afraid anymore. I could do anything again.

"Saving electricity?" she asked.

The Chair

I directed her to the main room light switch.

"You look like shit," she observed when she'd illuminated us. "Are you sick?"

I pushed my fingers through hair that was both greasy and dusty. I could smell myself.

"How come you're here?" I asked.

"Do you want me to go?"

"No," I said.

But maybe you should, I thought.

The chair was exactly where the delivery guys had left it, in the middle of the room, owning everything. It was conspicuously well-positioned, like the kids at the end of The Cat in the Hat, sitting at the window, with no trace of the carnage that had surrounded them seconds earlier. Here, however, the plastic that had covered the chair lay shredded and strewn about the floor. It was everywhere. It was so everywhere that I had to mention it to Hayley, saying how I didn't know how that had happened, but she said she'd seen mice do worse and that what I did in my own flat was my own business, especially over a weekend.

I stared at the visciously shredded plastic - overkill, I thought horribly - and then my eyes lingered on the ridge where the seat cushion met the bottom of the chair, a kind of mouth.

In a sing-song voice, Hayley said: "Nice chair."

Of course I thought that she was joking until she approached it and looked as though she might sit down.

It was perhaps deceptively comfortable-looking, but the idea of sitting in it was repulsive to me, even with Hayley in the room. Whereas it had seemed to be collapsing in on itself before, now it appeared to be standing firm on four scratched but strong, shapely legs.

Hayley circled it, looking it up and down, and then eyeing me the same way.

"You didn't get this chair for me, did you?" she said.

"I rescued it," I said.

My mouth fell open when she lay her bare hands on the seat back, resting her weight on it as she spoke to me.

"All the best things are rescued from some fate or other," she said.

I snapped my jaw shut again, because, seriously, what was I going to say? 'Don't touch my chair - it's dangerous?'

She was staring at me so intently that I wondered if I had something on my face.

"I like you," she said, as if she'd surprised herself.

"I like you too," I said. "And, Hayley, I'm not just saying that because you did."

"This isn't like me," she admitted. "To turn up like this."

"Do you want to talk in private?" I asked, feeling uncomfortable with the chair listening in.

She looked around at a room, full of just us.

"I could do with some air," I added.

"I just came to check that you're okay," Hayley said. "I can't stay, because I've got exams, but you could walk me back to the station?"

"I'd like you to stay," I said.

I'd almost said need. I had.

"Next time," she said.

As we left the flat, I thought I heard the chair sniggering to itself, but it could have been shredded plastic rustling against the bare boards. It was seriously everywhere, like the world's shittiest confetti.

The Chair

*

We stopped at a bench and she sat down. Before sitting beside her, I would normally have pretended to drop something so that I could get down on my knees to check that the bench was bolted to the ground. Even though I would have known that nothing bad was going to happen to me while she was around, I would have felt the need to check that the bench was tethered.

Tonight, after a really terrible weekend trapped in my kitchen, this bench didn't seem so bad. All chairs in the world had been tamed thanks to the wild thing I'd allowed into my flat. Hayley had been right. Facing one of my key fears might have destroyed my weekend, but it had made me stronger.

I fished my spare key out of my pocket and put it in her palm. She looked at me curiously, like I was rushing into things.

"Turn up after classes," I said. "Or if you just need to get away from home. Or for no reason at all."

She rested her head on my shoulder. I felt guilty though, because it wasn't a selfless act – I knew it would be good for her to have a key to my flat in case something happened to me.

She took the key and headed down the stairs to the platform. I kept walking, heading away from home. Pretending to be strong for Hayley had given me real strength to do something I would have convinced myself was impossible hours ago.

*

Aside from a light in an upstairs window, Charlie's house was in darkness. It had an otherworldy tinge, as if I'd lived a lifetime since I'd been here last, as if I'd died and come back but not all the way. I climbed the steps to the front door, feeling like I'd been deposited in an alternate reality.

The bell sounded just the same as always; an electronic chime that resonated deep inside the house. If the kitchen was the heart of this house - it always had been in the past, thanks to Jeanette's cooking - then I was standing at the mouth. It was either about to swallow me or spit me onto the street.

The familiarity of the doorstep, with the same potted plants on either side and dark blue, council paintwork, was not reassuring, as I had hoped it would be, but more like a lie spat in my face. No matter how much the house seemed the same, I knew that things would be irreparably different for those who lived within.

The first clear evidence that things had changed within was that it was Jeanette who flicked on the landing light and came to the door in the middle of the night to ask me what the hell I wanted; not Charlie. That was new.

She was wearing a purple shirt with the sleeves neatly folded up. She clenched the door jamb with one hand. I didn't know if she were deriving the strength to stand, or if she were trying to snap it in two. She eyed me like I was a ticking parcel on her doorstep.

Rather than invite me in, she stepped outside to join me. She used her free hand to pull the door almost shut behind her. There was just a slither of light coming out now.

"What are you doing here?" she asked brusquely.

This might have seemed rude if I hadn't almost killed her husband.

"I've come to see Charlie," I said.

She looked at me for so long without speaking that I thought maybe she had hit her head too.

"I've come to ap..."

"- Don't," she told me. "You needn't have come."

"I think I did," I countered. "Charlie's not answering his phone. You are. I just want to talk to him."

"Charlie doesn't want to see you."

"I believed that, months ago," I said, "but now I'd like to hear it from him."

Charlie's injury was the root of my fear. I had to face up to it, and him, if I were to have a chance at a normal life. I felt like I was close. Close to being almost normal again.

"He came out of your car a different man than he went in," Jeanette said. "The old Charlie's gone. You came out of the accident the same selfish cunt though."

There was no denying that all that was true, except I wouldn't have said that I came out of the accident unchanged.

"I need to see him," I said.

"Do you know, that's what you said the night you drove him into a tree," she said. "Those exact words."

No, I hadn't remembered that. Of course not.

"I need to see him. I need to see him. Like I'm some sort of gatekeeper. I didn't try to stop him going. He asked me to get rid of you. He didn't want to go with you."

"That's not true," I said.

"Ask him yourself then," she said, "I'm not stopping you. I'm just telling you that he doesn't want to see you. He didn't that night. And he doesn't now."

She stepped aside, so that I could go in.

It felt like a trap.

I found myself thinking of the accident very clearly now. I physically twisted my head around like I was back there, with the smell of petrol in my nose and Charlie's blood splashed on my face and clothes.

The chair - the leather interior that I'd been so impressed by - seemed to be crushing him against the dashboard, although really it was probably the other way round, but what I'd seen, what it had seemed like, what I remembered vividly now, was that the chair was killing him. I remember pulling at it and how he'd screamed. He'd screamed and a couple of teeth had fallen out.

The chair had tried to swallow him whole and he'd stopped screaming then, prepared to let it.

"Haven't you wondered why you never see him around?" she said. "You live in the same neighborhood! This is how you met. If he wanted to see you, he'd have done it.

"Do you have any idea what you've done to him? He never goes outside, Alan. He only leaves the house for appointments at the hospital and then I have to make him. It takes me an hour to convince him to put on his clothes. Sometimes I have to do it for him. I take him to the car and I drive him in and then I wait. I sit next to him, in the waiting room, in the doctor's office, in the chair next to his bed, and all the time I'm waiting, just waiting and waiting, I think about how much I hate you for what you've done to us."

Aside from a physical assualt, I noted, this was going about as badly as it could.

If Hayley had been there, she'd have known what to say or do, but I was me and I didn't. I hadn't thought this through. I was just bulldozering it, as usual. Jeanette was sort of right about me. 'It'll be alright' only gets you so far.

"I'm talking about looking someone you love in the eye and knowing that that person is gone," Jeanette said. "That person is shattered, like so much glass in the road.

"Well go on then!" she said, pushing the door open. "It's your turn to stare at him, though he won't thank me for

The Chair

letting you in."

I saw tears running down her face. It had this distant look as if it belonged to someone else and that other person was crying and snot was coming out of that other person's nose and it had nothing to do with her so she just let it happen, just let it hang there, swinging. Her tears made her eyes black.

I heard movement inside and my courage failed.

"Jeannette?" I heard a voice say from around the corner of the corridor. There was a thumping sound as Charlie came closer. "Who are you talking to?" He sounded drunk or sleepy.

I tripped down the steps and took off into the night. I didn't look back. I felt bad about that, but in the end I didn't want Charlie to see me until I was better prepared. Of course, it was possible that day might never come.

*

The chair didn't ambush me, although I'd been willing it to happen all the way home. It was sitting in the middle of the room, like it hadn't moved all weekend, like it hadn't got bored of waiting behind the door.

"I know what you're up to," I said. "It won't work. I know I'm not mad. And I'm not afraid of you."

Nothing. It was persisting with the act.

"You're a fucking ugly fucking bitch," I said, enunciating clearly, breathing hard from running up the stairs for this confrontation. "Did you hear me?" Admittedly, it didn't have anything identifiable as ears. Deaf. Dumb. Blind. Yet alive. Waiting.

"What for?" I said. "What are you waiting for?"

I stood like a cowboy facing down an opponent.

I went over to the beast and delivered it a kick in the lips. My trainer made a dull thump against it and I stumbled. I kicked it again, raising my knee high this time and slamming my heel into its face. It shunted across the floor, wheels grating. Still no retaliation.

"If you're going to do something, now's the time," I said.

I opened my arms wide, inviting the attack.

The chair sat very, very still.

"I'm going to piss on you," I announced. "I'm going to take my cock out and I'm going to piss on you." I started to do it, unzipping my fly. "I brought you here for a reason. So finish it. Do something! Do anything!"

"Alan?" Hayley said.

She was standing in the bedroom doorway, looking scared. She had my blue bathrobe wrapped around her.

I stuffed my cock back into my trousers.

"How long have you been standing there?"

"I wasn't sure if I should say anything or not, but at first it seemed like you were talking to me and then you seemed to be talking to the chair, so ... I said something and if you want me to leave, I'm out of here."

"I didn't know you were here," I said. "You weren't meant to hear any of that."

She didn't look reassured.

"What are you doing here?"

"I waited for the train, but I felt like I was being drawn here again. Like you needed me."

"I do."

"So I let myself in and you weren't here, which was a surprise, and I thought I'd surprise you by climbing into your bed. So ... surprise. Okay. So I'm going to leave now."

The Chair

"No! Wait."

A tremor crossed her face.

"I'm not going to hurt you!" I said.

She looked at her clothes on the bed, and then looked at the door, making calculations.

"You said I could tell you anything. 'Any time' you said. Well, I've got something to tell you. And I'd better do it now, because it looks like I might not get another chance."

"Can I sit down for this?" Hayley asked warily.

"Better not," I said, and then I told her. "You see ... I've got this fear. A phobia."

"Chairs?" she said.

I felt cold enough to merit going straight to bed without finishing this conversation.

"Yes. And I know that might sound ridiculous," I said, "but do you know what it's like to live with a phobia?"

"I was scared of spiders once," she said. "You wouldn't have got me sitting on your floor – or doing anything else down there - a couple of years ago."

Apparently you're always within arm's length of a spider, but at least you're not alone in your fear - it's one of the most common phobias in the world. I wish I could have been afraid of spiders instead of chairs.

"My mom said that when I was a kid, about four years old, we were walking through the woods and I got spider web in my hair. The web was full of these tiny, spider babies and they were running all over my head, making my scalp itch, and they started tickling their way down my neck and over my face. I was scratching like mad, but my brother said that the mummy spider was following us home and that at night, when everyone went to bed, she was going to crawl into my room to get her kids back and she'd be furious about the babies I'd killed by scratching, so I just let them crawl all over me; I cried all the way home and all night. I was pretty hysterical by the morning and I had the fear all my life."

"That's pretty fucking terrifying for a four year old," I said.

"Apparently, whenever I heard something creaking on the floor or tapping on the window, I thought it was the mummy spider trying to get in. Whenever I saw a spider, I asked my mum to kill them, so they couldn't tell their mummy where I was, but I always felt like the mummy spider was out there somewhere, just getting angrier and angrier, and bigger and bigger, and hungrier and hungrier and that she was making a big web in a tree just for me so that when she found me she could drag me there and hang me up and let me starve and let her little kiddies feed on me."

"That's ... fucked ... up," I said. "How did you get over it?"

"As I got older, I didn't know why I was so scared of spiders. I just knew I hated them and that they had to die. I felt like I'd die if they were allowed to live. I used to cut my hair dead short and people thought I was a punk, and I sort of got convinced it suited me for a while too. I only remembered why I was scared of spiders, particularly of having them in my hair, because mum told me about it after I admitted I was thinking about seeing a hypnotherapist. The fear went away. Overnight."

I smiled at the idea of waking up one day without fear.

"One crawled right over my bedsheets a few nights later and I let it live. In the morning, neither of us were dead and I was completely cured. That's the power of talking things over with the right people."

The Chair

My mouth was dry, like a big, dusty cave. With a giant spider under a rock.

"Some kind of trauma is often the root of a phobia."

"Yeah ... I know that ... but I can't just ..."

It nearly slipped out.

"So, you're afraid of chairs?" Hayley said, tilting her head to one side.

"Yeah," I murmured.

She pursed her lips and seemed to be trembling.

"Are you okay?" I said.

She burst out laughing then. She laughed like a lunatic, with her shoulders going and gasping for breath, bent over, as if it ached her chest and stomach and sides to laugh so hard, but she couldn't stop.

"Shit," she said, wheezing. "I'm sorry." She glanced up at me and however I looked sent her into hysterics again. I thought she might collapse and start kicking her legs.

I was on a knife edge then. Either I was going to start laughing too and we'd hold each other and start fucking, or I was going to haul her out of here and throw her into the corridor.

For a second, I could imagine hating her and that scared me. I could almost see myself slapping her and telling her to go and not come back. I didn't want to live that version. The version where I'd died in the car crash would have been better than that.

"Please," I whispered.

"That's why you've got no chairs," she said. "Are you for real? How do you function at work? Or on the bench earlier?"

"Nothing ever happens if someone else is around."

"Happens? Like what? What 'happens'?"

"I don't think ... I don't think you get to laugh anymore," I said. "You'll notice that I'm not laughing."

"I'm sorry," she said. "But one day, we'll be laughing about this. Together. I promise you we will."

"... they want to kill me," I said.

"Why would anything want to kill you?"

"Because I saw one of them murdering someone and I wasn't meant to see, but I did - there was a lot of blood and it must have lost control - so now I know about them and I know that sounds insane, but ... They don't all want to kill me. Some of them just want to be near me. But I don't want that. I don't want to be killed. Or near them. Not when they're moving."

"How long has this been going on?"

"Since my car crash. I hit my head, but I got checked out. Apparently, I'm fine. You don't look convinced though."

"You're right," said Hayley. "This doesn't sound fine."

I admired the way she stood there, barefoot and naked beneath the robe, listening to me talk about chairs that want to kill me.

"I realise that hearing someone say all this shit might be unnerving," I said, "and if you want to leave now, you can. I'll stand over there and you can let yourself out and we can talk about it tomorrow. Or never. No hard feelings."

"I'm not going anywhere," she said, holding my gaze steady. "If you need me ..."

"... I do ..."

"... I'm here for you. But is there anything else you need to tell me?"

I pushed an elbow towards the armchair.

"That chair wasn't for you. I brought it up here from

out in the street to desensitize myself. Kind of a brute force approach, because I wanted to do it fast, before I saw you again actually."

"I think you might have bitten off more than you could chew with that one," she said, eyeing it.

I shuddered.

"This is what you've been writing in your journal," she said.

Things were falling into place for her. My lost weekend. Our failed date at the cinema which had happily ended in a pile of clothes on the floor of this very room.

"You don't need to impress me," she said. "And you're not going to scare me off." She wrapped her arms around me and, having stood there like a dead thing, I melted into her hug. I was liquid when she caressed my face. "You're going to be fine," she said. "You don't deserve this. You're a good person. A bit weird, okay? But interesting. And good."

I laughed; something I wouldn't have thought possible a few minutes ago.

She offered to make me a drink, but I asked her to go into the bedroom and wait for me. I wanted a moment alone with my thoughts.

Secretly, I wanted a minute or two with the chair.

The bedroom door went click.

"Tomorrow you go back on the street," I warned the chair quietly, "out the window if necessary, so if you're going to do something, now's your chance."

The chair didn't twitch, but I got the impression it was sulking with me, like if I wasn't prepared to play by its rules then it wasn't prepared to play at all.

"You're not moving and I'm not afraid, so I should be cured," I said, "but I don't feel cured. Why do I feel like this isn't over yet?"

That's when I heard laughter and the chair no longer looked like a ragged, threadbare item of furniture, but an alien creature with permanently broken wings, four legs all facing the wrong way so that any attempt to move at speed ought to tear the creature apart, and several pairs of lips, wherever there was darkness between folds. With all this going on at once, it made no physical move, but I heard a deep laugh come from inside it, like the chugging of a distant train.

Then, through the open window, came the wooshing sound of the sliding doors at the main entrance. A second sound marked someone's entrance to the foyer. My hairs stood on end. Then the doors slid shut again.

There'd been an accompanying sound that I didn't recognise at all, but that I knew shouldn't have been in the building. It was wrong. While I tried to place it, I heard another unfamiliar sound from the end of the hall, but I knew what this sound was.

The lift was working.

The doors opened for the first time since I'd moved into the flat. I'd not heard any workmen around recently and I'd been home, in the kitchen, the whole time. They'd been no notices to say that the lift was being repaired. And yet I heard the doors trundle open with an accompanying hiss, as though it had decided to start working again all by itself.

Instead of footsteps, I heard that whirring sound again. As it drew nearer, I noted again that it sounded like a bicycle, as though someone were riding down the hall.

The chair chuckled. I'd thought I was over being afraid, but there was a chapter yet to play out.

Predictably, disturbingly, the whirring, tinkling,

The Chair

humming sound stopped outside my door and then the flat seemed very, very quiet as if everything nearby were holding its breath.

"Who is it?" I asked the chair.

Whoever it was thumped against the door, just once, hard enough to make the letterbox rattle.

It was a thump that said: "I know you're in there."

"Charlie?" I whispered.

The chair chuckled again.

I felt that this was a final test. I was afraid, but I was up to the challenge the chairs were laying down for me, whatever it was.

Even so, as I approached the door, my legs were weak and had the idea of maybe waiting out whatever was out there. I could just go to bed and whoever it was would tire and go away. I could deal with the fallout in the morning, in daylight, which wasn't all that far away. Except that Hayley was here and, like before, I sensed that if I wanted to keep her, I had to deal with my issues, real or imagined.

I had to open the door.

Every part of me was shaking.

"Who is it?" I asked again, addressing the person him or herself this time.

There was no vocal answer, only another thump on the door, reminiscent of a forehead splitting against a dashboard. The metal letterbox cover clattered.

I supposed that Hayley must have been asleep, because she didn't come out to see what was going on. Given my appearance - my body trembling and sweaty, my mouth and eyes wide open - I wanted her to stay where she was.

I had to open the door to stop the noise bringing Hayley out here.

My heart was beating so loud that it seemed more audible than my footsteps as I crept towards the door.

I put my eye to the peephole.

There was nobody standing outside. Instead, I saw the door opposite mine, with something casting a shadow on the wood. I swallowed hard.

As far as I could see, the corridor to the left and right appeared to be empty.

I worked up the courage to slowly tease open the letterbox cover. It meant pushing my fingers through bristles intended to keep out the draft. It was like sliding my hand into a moustached mouth.

I felt the tip of the cover against my fingers and pushed.

This time, instead of being able to see the door oppoisite, something obstructed my view. It was not a person but an object of some sort.

When I felt brave enough to unlock the door, long after looking through the letterbox, I undid the latch.

In the hallway, settled expectantly in front of my door, was an empty wheelchair.

*

Gingerly, I glanced up and down the hall to see if the wheelchair's intentions had been inhibited by the presence of an observer, but no, it was just me and the chair out there.

It appeared to be relatively new. Not like an old lady wheelchair. It was all leather and chrome and the wheels might have been described as alloys. I would have approved of it in my flashy, car-racing days.

Unlike the armchair behind me, the wheelchair looked as if it were still in service. I didn't find myself

The Chair

imagining it discarded at the side of the road, or throwing itself out of a skip and clattering to the gutter before trying to right itself unobserved. Whereas I'd imagined that the armchair might be the last of its kind, I saw the wheelchair as one of a multitude, much like the office chairs or the cinema seats. It was the vangaurd in an army that had turned its attention towards me.

"What does it want?" I asked the armchair. "What do you want?" I asked the wheelchair.

No movement now. No sign of sentience.

My door was marked low down where the wheelchair had bashed into it. If it rolled forward suddenly now it would get me in the ankles. If it were vicious enough, it could probably break them and then I'd be down on the floor, crawling across the room while wheels ran over my hands and legs.

Despite my paralysing apprehension, no attack came. This appeared to be a growing trend. Admittedly, it was one that I didn't trust.

My bedroom door was still shut and all seemed still within. Satisfied, I let the front door swing all the way open and I stood back.

The wheelchair didn't enter. Instead, the footrests flopped down and clacked into position. The sound echoed out in the empty hallway.

"You want me to sit in you?" I said. "No fucking way."

Even as my hand touched the front door to close it, I knew that the new chair would not be dissuaded that easily. It would jam itself between the door and the jamb, or, perhaps worse, it would sit out there forever, maybe rolling itself at the front door until I gave in or Hayley came out.

Hayley would think that I'd been making all this noise myself.

"You know what?" she'd say. "I might not be able to deal with this after all. I need some time."

"Okay," I told the wheelchair.

I didn't feel about the wheelchair the way I felt about the armchair. It wasn't full of hate or malice or spiteful glee. It wasn't hungry for me - for my dead skin, for my stale air. It was still sort of, chair-like. It hadn't been on the planet long enough to morph into something with that otherness and potential for animal ferocity that older chairs had.

Nonetheless, I approached it slowly and put my hand on its cool, leather-clad arm. No electric shock. No pulse. It was the way I would have expected it to feel if somebody had been watching me do this. It just felt like an ordinary chair.

I turned my back to it, so I could lower myself into its black leather seat. Inside my apartment, the dirty great armchair watched. It seemed to be smirking, as if it knew something that I didn't yet know. The way I understood it, chairs could communicate with each other, or rather they shared a kind of hive mind, so it did know something I didn't. No doubt it knew many things that I did not know, could not know and would never know. The important thing for me, however, was that that didn't scare me anymore. Not like before. I literally had Hayley in my corner. As long as I remembered that, I would be unbreakable.

There was a creaking sound as I sat gently in the seat, and then again as I raised my feet and put them on the footplates. With that, the wheelchair turned violently ninety degrees and I tried to get up but I was pushed back into the seat by the speed with which we were rolling down the hall towards the lift.

The Chair

That humming sound of tyres on tiles again.

The lift doors opened for us and we went in.

There was nobody at reception at this time of the morning, so we whirred straight past the desk with nobody to see that no-one was pushing the chair and that it wasn't automated.

"Where are we going?" I asked, but I thought that I knew.

The sliding doors hissed open and we hit the street.

*

We took back streets primarily so nobody would see us, bumping up and down pavements and juddering over cracks, navigating the holes in the road. I was just in my shirt and jeans and the chilly air brought goosebumps all over my flesh.

The first time the chair stopped dead I thought that I was supposed to get up, but it turned out that it was only letting people pass so that we could the pass unnoticed. Each time we stopped, the chair started again of its own accord and we would slip by, unseen though perhaps heard, whirring through the night.

We passed the underground and then Charlie and Jeanette's place, so I was out of ideas regarding our destination.

In one dark fantasy the wheelchair took me to my office building and the sliding doors opened up automatically, just like they had at my flat except this time the wheelchair dumped me on the floor and when I looked up I found myself in a room full of blue swivel chairs. They glared at me with desire as their ranks closed in, rolling, shuffling, wobbling, juddering. I was the reward for their patience.

When we reached a busy intersection of road, the chair halted at a zebra crossing and I had to wheel myself across because people were watching from their cars. I put my hands on the handrims and pushed. Gaining momentum wasn't difficult, because the chair was assisting; all I had to do was look the part. The chair controlled the speed and the direction, all the way to the grand, stone archway that marked the main entrance to the hospital, all the way through the busy front car park and on towards the main entrance.

Inside the busy reception area, I squinted against the glare of the lights burning above. There were rows of chairs, marking waiting areas for different facillities. The wheelchair skirted its cousins and rushed us towards a lift.

Nearby, two drunk girls were arguing about who had won the fight that had sent them both to hospital. They were planning to settle this outside once they were patched up. Everybody within earshot of them was either watching, joining in or pretending not to listen, which meant that the wheelchair was able to whisk me into the lift without anybody noticing. Everybody was somehow involved in the escalating argument, except for Jeanette, who I spotted looking weary as she retrieved a coffee from a vending machine.

Her face was blank and made me think of a beaten pillow, plumped up for appearances but essentially lifeless. Her features were drawn and cords stood out on her neck, as if she had been stretched and then allowed to shrink back to normal size with all the skin just hanging around.

She wasn't interested in the brawling girls' argument and she was in no state of mind to notice me. If she was here then it was because Charlie had had to come in. Her attention was absorbed by his needs. Perhaps it always had been. It was

The Chair

a perfect illustration of how wrong about her I'd been. I'd been wrong about a lot of things.

The lift doors opened and closed without my intervention and we went up to the 6th floor.

The last time I'd been here, Jeanette had had to be restrained. Meanwhile, security had escorted me out of the building for my own safety. One of the guys had pushed me, even though I'd recently been in a car crash. I hadn't complained though. I deserved more than that. Charlie had been unconscious, having had his face caved in a twisted combination of my car, a metal crash barrier and a tree.

The smell of the ward was just as it had been that night, which caused my body to respond accordingly. I gripped the flesh of the armrests and curled my toes in my trainers, latching onto the wheelchair as it carried me along. The ward didn't smell clean to me. Apparently it was a kind of disinfectant that made this odour, but it wasn't the kind of thing I'd ever used in my kitchen or bathroom. This stuff smelled like sickness itself and gave me the impression that cleaners had smeared the dirt and germs around into an invisible paste that was on every surface, in every corner, under every bed.

As the wheelchair rolled up the sparse corridor, I looked in through any doors that were open. I saw people in various states of disrepair. Some of them were sitting up, though they had tubes up their noses and were connected to machines. Their eyes flicked over at me for the brief time in which I featured in their doorway, but no other part of them ever moved.

Charlie was going to be behind one of these doors. I had to prepare myself for the possibility that he wouldn't move. I had to prepare myself for the possibility that he'd be dead.

The chair reached the end of the corridor and entered the last room on the left.

I sat stiffly in the chair like a prisoner that had reached the moment of liberation or execution. There was no time for a final request, although that would have been to see Hayley again, just for a few more years. Instead there was time only for a few words - from me to him and perhaps from him to me.

The wheelchair rolled to a very gentle stop and then the handbrakes thudded into position.

Charlie, if this was indeed Charlie, hadn't heard us come in. He lay on his back beneath the covers. Like everyone else up here, he was connected to a machine. A tube extended from a clear bag on a stand and disappeared underneath the crips white bedsheets, presumably entering his arm.

I pushed myself up from the chair and allowed the circulation to return my legs before moving unsteadily across the room and looking down at a very pale man with a bloated, asymetrical face.

Not Charlie, I'd thought at first.

This isn't Charlie, I'd hoped.

His face was a lattice of scars, but one in particular drew the eye. It went across his forehead so that he was permanently frowning. I'd heard about this scar. Mutual acquiantances would talk about him, but stop when they realised that a) I'd been driving the car or b) I hadn't visited him since the accident.

They'd sort of shut up then and look uncomfortable and confused.

"Maybe you should go and see him," they'd said. "I'm

sure he'd appreciate that."

I'd tried not to laugh at their optimism.

"I will," I'd replied every time, but instead, I'd relived the moments after the crash. I'd recall the memory of talking to a half-dead Charlie, trying to keep him alive so that my survival could be justified.

Now, once again, I felt myself staring at him in the hope that he was still alive. His breaths were so shallow that I could have been imagining them. I thought of taking a pulse from his neck, but I didn't dare touch him. I didn't think I had the right to do that. And I didn't want him to wake up to find my fingers against his throat. I preferred to just stand there for an hour and see if he moved.

While I waited, I remembered his voice. Earlier this evening, at Jeanette's, he'd sounded sleepy. In the car, after the accident, he'd sounded like he was gargling blood. Even though I thought he'd die for sure, I'd told him that help was coming and that if he held on everything was going to be okay. I'd been much stronger then. The first lie had been powerful enough to keep him alive. Subsequently, I'd been lying to myself for months, but they'd lost their power.

I no longer lied to myself that keeping Charlie conscious had been my instinct. My first impulse had been to finish him off, as he'd seemed to be begging me to, but I hadn't had the guts. His right eye had come loose from its socket. I'd thought it was going to fall right out. I'd been fixated on it, my instinct to catch it rather than lose it in the wreckage of the car. I imagined his eye being taken away with the car to be crushed into a box and disposed of, finishing the job that my trajectory into a barrier had started. It seemed really important not to let his eye get thrown away, no matter what happened to the rest of him.

His face had seemed to be dissolving. The smell of his blood made me gag and there was the odour of spilled petrol and oil and smoke and though I knew what that combination meant I couldn't just leave him there and so I'd stayed, trying to find a way to get him out that didn't involve looking at him or touching him, trying to think of the right things to say, wondering why I wasn't even hurt.

And then I saw the seat move by itself. It shunted forwards forcefully and I thought that maybe another car had hit us, but no, it was the seat. It had come dislodged from its mooring and, while I watched and screamed, it shoved Charlie forward, up over the dashboard and toward the twisted frame of the windscreen. Then it sank its ... its no teeth into Charlie's thigh.

He was too far gone to scream, but I wasn't.

The seat was crushing. Peeling. Feasting. It wasn't long before it was covered in Charlie's blood. It had looked as if it had been drinking it, swallowing, choking, laughing.

Charlie had hung on to life for Jeanette, even though the crash had opened his body in a dozen locations and even though the chair was intent on destroying all that was left of him, its raptorous intent revealed since it could no longer resist its true nature drenched in Charlie's blood.

It had been slurping, biting, tearing and even as it had done so Charlie had looked at me and we'd shared a moment across the terrible, bloody truth of the car's crushed interior. The crash wasn't going to kill him, but the chair was going to finish what I'd started.

Charlie was the only person on the planet who might have some idea of what I was going through.

Eventually, someone had rescued me, not from the

The Chair

car but from Charlie, dragging me out of the twisted space where the driver's side window had been.

"I'm fine!" I kept telling the paramedics, but they insisted on bringing me back here in an ambulance. Charlie arrived hours later, because it had taken that long to cut him free of the dashboard, and tree and chair.

*

When I opened my eyes, back on the 6th floor with the wheelchair that had brought me here, Charlie was awake. He had a good eye and a bad eye now. The good eye - dark blue like a starlit sky - held mine. The other pointed elsewhere, foggy and grey.

He didn't recognise me, but I was sure I looked less changed than he did. Forever, I'd associate this new, smaller, paler, child's drawing of Charlie with that weirdly, dirty hospital smell that lingered around him, punctuated by the smell from those squeezy bottles by the doors, the smell of too little too late.

His mouth twitched. I couldn't tell what that meant.

"I'll leave if you want," I told him.

"How long have you been here?" he said.

He didn't sound like the Charlie I remembered. I could have put that down to the fact that he was just waking up, but I'd run out places to hide things. I was tipping it all out on the floor. I knew that he was slurring and lisping, because a team of people had spent months putting his face back together and that the job wasn't finished yet, perhaps it never would be, like a kid's jigsaw with the pieces lost underneath Grandma's sofa, down between the cushions.

His breath, which had been easy, light and inaudible, now sounded like the sweeping of Autumn leaves out of the road, a laborious job that was never quite finished.

Seeking encouragement, I glanced at the wheelchair that had facilitated this meeting. It showed no signs of life now that Charlie was awake. It had done it's part and it was up to me to make the most of this opportunity.

"Charlie, I'm so sorry," I said. I was fucking crying. Like he needed to see that.

His biggest scar moved. So that's what a frown looked like now, I supposed.

"I know that doesn't change anything," I said.

"What do you want, Alan?" he said. "You always want something." Jeanette's words coming out of Charlie's broken, glued-up mouth. "What do you want? Does Jeanette know you're here?"

"She's downstairs. She didn't see me."

"You should go before she comes back."

All kinds of things I could have said came to mind. Stuff about how if I could have changed places with him, I would have done. How I walked away from the crash without a single injury and how unfair that was and how sorry I was about the universe's decision to spin it like that. How I wished I could have died if it meant that he would be okay. But all the words sounded like they were out of the movies.

"If you've finished gawking," Charlie said, "I'm going back to sleep."

"Charlie ... I ..."

"There's no point you being here," Charlie said, head back on the pillow, eyes closed. Raising his voice was causing him pain, as if breaking the cobwebs in his throat were like tearing flesh. "Words can't do anything. You can't do anything. So go! If you got what you wanted, go do whatever it is you've been doing; living, dying, lying, I don't

The Chair

give a fuck."

The word 'fuck' was followed by a coughing fit.

I wanted to ask him about the chair that had been eating him in the car, but I decided against it. He probably didn't remember and if he did he wouldn't want to. There was nothing more to gain here. I'd apologised.

"What I said about Jeanette," I said finally. "Obviously it wasn't true. She wasn't using you. She loved you."

"Why do you say that?" Charlie asked. "Because only someone who truly loved me could stand to look at me now?"

"No."

"Then why?"

"... Okay. Yes."

"Get out Alan."

I turned my muddle-mouth away from him, which is when I saw the prosthetic legs in the corner of the room. One was a flesh-coloured shin and calf, with metallic rods where the ankle should have been and a smooth black foot, like those things that are used to keep the shape of unworn shoes. The other was the same, but there was a knee and part of a thigh as well. It was all very futuristic.

They were standing up, the right foot next to the left foot, like a pair of polished shoes.

I noticed that there was empty space under the bedsheets where his legs should have been.

"Charlie, I didn't know."

"That I lost my legs? That's old news, Alan. I lost more than that. I lost everything. Everything but Jeanette."

I wanted to say that he still had me, but I knew that I shouldn't. Not only did he not want someone like me in his life - the person who had tried to separate him from the only person who really did love him - but I never wanted to see him again. Not really. Not like this.

But I'd done it. And while I felt more guilty now, not less, I no longer had that nagging feeling that I should be doing more. Jeanette and Charlie didn't want me anywhere near them and I was going to live out my life fulfilling their wishes.

I expected to sleep soundly, whether Hayley was still in my bed or not.

I should have been cured.

The Chair

EARLY, TUESDAY MORNING

I'd left the door open, so I walked straight in. The armchair was beside the window, but facing the front door. A good spot for it.

I didn't turn on the lights. The sun was coming up and light was beginning to filter in through the window.

I went first to the bedroom and saw that Hayley had gone.

"Fuck."

Last night could have been the start of something really special, but I'd had to leave. I'd had to go with the chair, otherwise I'd still be afraid. Perhaps I would always have been afraid.

I walked right up to my armchair in the growing light. I was weary and it was in the best spot in the room.

"I'm sitting down," I said.

It made a sound of disagreement, an internal rumble like a motorbike climbing a distant hill.

"Shut up," I said. "I own you. Not the other way round."

Sitting down heavily, the chair shifted uncomfortably beneath me.

"Stop! fucking! moving!" I said.

It did.

I allowed every part of my back to touch the

seatback.

As unpleasant as this was, as cold and damp as it felt wriggling and breathing unneccessarily against me, it was better than seeing Charlie's reconstituted face and the neat bedsheets stretched over nothing at the foot of his bed, his new legs standing beside the wall.

The worst chair in the world was the one that had crushed my friend half to death. The best chair was the wheelchair that substituted his legs and had come to tell me so. This big, dirty, stinking armchair was somewhere in the middle.

It was surprisngly comfortable once I got over the unpleasantness of actually touching it. I considered all the people who'd ever sat in it. I wondered if it knew who they were; if it had an internal guest book of arses and backs.

I chuckled to myself as I prised my phone out of my pocket. There was no message from Hayley, so I called up her name and tapped out a new message.

"Too much wierd for one night? I'm sorry. I went for a walk, but I was hoping you'd be here when I got back. I'd like to see you again. I hope you're okay." There was just room to add: 'I love u' with no full stop afterwards, but I deleted it. It was something I'd have to show her, not tell her. Starting from now.

I hit 'send'.

Within a couple of seconds, there was a beeping sound and the chair seat buzzed dully as something vibrated deep inside. The sensation was too rhythmic to be one of the chair's grumbles. I could actually sense that the chair was in quite a good mood, even though I was sitting in it. The noise - the pulse - had been electronic.

After that realisation, there was an awful stillness.

The Chair

The buzzing had stopped and the chair was playing dead, but loving the tension.

I felt as though I were paralysed, able only to move my thumb, re-entering my conversations, bringing up Hayley's number and pressing dial, hoping that I didn't feel anything.

My phone made a long 'boop' sound to signal that it was connected and a moment later I heard Hayley's ringtone coming from beneath me accompanied by buzzing deep down within the belly of the chair. I hung up and it was a second or two before the plastic case of Hayley's phone stopped rattling against the interior of the chair.

The chair was silent, like it was about to burst out laughing, but it knew it had done something terrible.

Looking around the room, I saw the blood for the first time. Not all of it. Just here and there. There was an odd mark on the back of the door. The wood was severely dented and there was a dark patch that I couldn't see clearly from my sitting position but could have been wet. Although it was dark, it sort of glistened.

Likewise, I noticed blood on the floor. I'd walked in it without noticing because it was dark and there wasn't that much blood. It was a line of droplets, nothing too dramatic, except that the trail of blood - which sounded worse, so I stuck with it being a line of droplets - the line of droplets was going from the doorway to where I was sitting. The fact that there was any blood at all was alarming, but more so was that one end of the line stopped at the chair.

I spotted blood on the wall beside the door. Low down, suggesting crawling. Then it has been smeared, suggesting dragging. I was no detective, so I couldn't really say that Hayley had been thrown against it and crushed and then dragged away. I couldn't say that for certain.

Nothing else was out of place.

"So, you've got her phone," I said out loud.

"I'm going to reach in and get it," I said, half disbelieving myself.

I pushed my fingers down between the leather seat cushion and the inside of the arm.

It wasn't damp. It was wet. The chair had been out in the rain but that was several days ago. This wasn't damp caused by rain. It could have been sweat, or saliva. It was dark down there.

My fingers kept reaching ghost shapes and I'd draw my hand away and see that my fingers were red, but I pushed them back in, pushing hard so that eventually my palm was completely inside the chair and then my wrist was too, feeling around inside some internal cavity.

It was also wet or slimy in here and I was afraid of a mouth closing around my arm, but perhaps that was what I deserved. Charlie had lost his legs because of me, I could lose an arm. I didn't know if that would start to make us even, but that was part of the reason I kept on, wanting to feel pain. That was part of it.

When half of my forearm was submerged inside the chair, my fingertips came across something solid. I accidentally pushed whatever it was deeper into the chair, but I did my best to steady my hand and spread my fingers to trap the object. I couldn't grip it too hard, because it was slippery, but once I had a decent hold on it, I drew it out slowly.

Sure enough, I was looking at Hayley's mobile phone. It didn't show any signs of damage, except for the blood on screen.

"What did you do?" I said.

The Chair

I set the phone on my knee, while I pushed my hand back into the chair, reaching down, down, down between the cushion and the arm, sliding my forearm between cold, wet lips. My fingers probed the fleshy blackness that my eyes could not see; the hairy, oozing fabric-lined belly of the chair.

There was a framework for sure. My hands kept tugging at things that didn't move. It was coathangers and teeth and a skeleton all at once. It was forgotten things and hidden objects. It was the horde of a lifetime, slowly dissolving into dust.

At full extension, with my cheek squashed against the leather arm, my middle finger came across something that gave when I touched it. After a few attempts, I managed to pinch the object between my index finger and thumb and draw it up until I could use my entire hand to get a grip around it. Whatever it was, it was big. Too big to go sliding down the side of a chair accidentally.

It wasn't hard like a mobile phone, but malleable, so that I got the impression that it was bending as I dislodged it from its resting place. I wriggled it, bicep and lungs burning, my face aching from my grimace.

Eventually, the object came free, and I suspect that the chair gave it up with a cough. I was able to reaffirm my grip on it, with dread, with my stomach convulsing and my throat burning. My heart was thumping inside my body, begging me to stop.

I knew what it would be.

I didn't need to pull it all the way out.

I'd dislodged a foot. It was the toes I'd pinched between my fingers moments ago. The nails were tourquoise.

Biting back a scream, I hauled on the foot and it came out more easily than I'd anticipated, because the chair had let go of it now and because it wasn't attached to anything else. It ended at the ankle. There was a ring of blood where the calf should have been; fraying flesh and smashed bone.

I threw it across the room and leapt from the chair at the same time. The foot hit the floor with a thud and skidded to a stop at the skirting board. It stopped like a dead, alien thing, half curled up and bloody.

Behind me, the chair actually giggled. It was a hag, this chair. A kindly old woman with silver hair who only ever opened the door a crack, because there were people swinging from the ceiling inside and she wanted to get back to talking to them.

"Fuck you!" I screamed at it. I waited to wake up in my bed, hoping that I was in a fucked up coma or something, but I didn't wake, I just stood there feeling myself yelling: "Fuck you! Fuck you!" with spit flying from my mouth, knowing that no-one would ever believe that I hadn't killed her and chopped her up and stuffed her down into the chair and then sat there like a fucking lunatic checking for messages from her.

"Why did you do that?" I yelled.

It moved, like a shrug.

My eyes went from the chair to the severed foot. Was she still in there? Had it digested the rest of her? Those bone-like things that I hadn't been able to budge - had they not been the chair at all, but Hayley's body? Her ribs? A broken spine?

The bottom of the chair seemed to be bulging more than usual, bloated, a distended gut on castors.

I'd invited it in here, thinking I was traumatised. I'd given Hayley a key, thinking that I'd be cured. I practically fed her to it.

I'd wanted her to be right about how people could

The Chair

overcome their fears and get their lives back. I wanted that to be true so badly that I'd stopped believing my own senses. I hadn't noticed the torn curtains, nor the blood on the wall where it had chased and perhaps caught her. Maybe she'd been thinking about throwing herself out of the window. Maybe she'd been in the process of doing just that when the chair had caught her by that foot and dragged her back into the room.

"You shouldn't have done it," I said.

The chair shrugged its shoulders again. Horrible.

My phone buzzed in my pocket.

I supposed that I should call the police. There was no point running or trying to hide from this. That much I'd learned.

Charlie was calling.

I put him on loudspeaker.

"Alan," he began with a deep, rattling sigh. "I shouldn't have said what I did earlier. My pain meds were wearing off."

"That's okay," I said. "Goodbye, Charlie."

"Wait. I wanted to say that I've gone through what I've gone through and you're going through what you're going through and it's not easy for any of us. I don't really blame you. We've all got shit to deal with."

"Yeah," I said. "That's incredibly generous, Charlie, but I don't really deserve this."

"We're alive, Alan, and that's what counts. We've got to make the best of what we've got and appreciate every moment we can. That's all there is to it. Life's too short to hold onto the past. And life's too short to beat yourself up about an accident. You've got to hold on to the people close to you."

"That sounds like fantastic advice Charlie. Except, I should have died in the crash. I saw something and I think seeing it made it real. I think I brought something into the world, Charlie. I've made bad things happen. If I'd died, you'd have been okay. Jeanette too. Hayley would have been okay."

"It's over," Charlie said soothingly, like putting a plaster on a severed limb.

The chair coughed something else up. My journal flopped to the floor as one solid mass, like a dead fish.

I didn't hear the moment Charlie hung up the phone. I imagined instead the whirring sound of his wheels and the slap of his hands on the grips as he went back to his life, such as I'd left it.

I picked up the journal and wiped blood from the current page so I could write.

I wrote automatically. It's important not to overthink things when you're trying to get your emotions onto the page.

"They're everywhere," I wrote. "We might not be watching them, but they're watching us. Some of them help us. Others kill the people we love and then laugh in our faces."

I glanced at the door and the chair emitted a creaking clicking sound, as if it were telling me that I'd never make it if I tried to run.

Tut-tut-tut.

Tut-tut-fucking-tut.

"Not all chairs are bad," I wrote. "This one is ... I got the chair I deserved."

I underlined the last sentence, my pen going through the damp page and through the next one and definitively tearing the one beneath that.

The Chair

The End

About This Story

When my interest in dreams and nightmares became more of a hobby than a passing interest, I started a Yahoo! group where people could share their stories. There were some fascinating characters with great stories. I recall chatting with a witch. And a Vietnam veteran joined, saying: "Oh yeah, I have nightmares ... a lot of nightmares ..."

Some people I met in that group are friends to this day. Others came and went. I've not been able to get in touch with the guy who gave me the seed of the story you've just read.

He told me that he once had a phobia about chairs. He thought that they could move and think and that they wanted to do him harm. If you look at almost any chair, you can see a mouth.

Now sit on that in the knowledge that it wants to bite.

I asked him how he survived on a day to day basis and he said he learned to manage his fears. It was only an issue when he was alone with a chair or chairs. As long as there were other people, or the chairs or seats were fixed, as in a cinema or on the bus, then he was fine.

"I'm so sorry," I said. "But, you know, tell me EVERYTHING."

I asked him if I could write a story about it one day and he very kindly said yes.

If you're the guy who told me this story, please get in touch. Thank you for the idea. I'm glad you're ending was better than Alan's.

The Chair

To everyone else: I'm glad I've had the opportunity to share this story with you. It might make you think twice before you sit down.

About the Author

Dean Clayton Edwards writes in the South of France with his wife and two daughters.

He has a writing chair in the attic.

For more, |check out http://deanclaytonedwards.com

Acknowledgements

I can't mention everyone who helps me to write and to write better, but I'd like to give a special mention to my beta readers.

Thanks to author Peter Torvell for your prompt responses and for providing useful insights. Merel Bel, it's great to have you on board and thank you for volunteering your valuable opinions.

Wendy Waring, thank you for giving up a writing session to talk about my story with me, and Christine Higdon, your input was beyond my expectations and I'm very grateful.

Enasha de Zoysa, you're a natural at this and I'm glad we found that out. And Claire Charlesworth. You 'got' some of my favorite bits and I appreciate the balance of your feedback.

A special thank you to Andy Harper for taking my cover image, having fun wth it, and helping it to tell this story.

Marianne. I have a favorite story about filmmaker editing the final reel of his movie while it is showing in the cinema several blocks across town. He races through the streets, charges through the doors and takes the stairs two at a time to deliver the last reel to the projectionist just in time so that the audience doesn't know that anything happened. The movie continues and the reel falls to pieces on the floor.

I can't remember who it was. It could have been

Kubrick. I kind of hope it was. Anyway, in my personal version of this story, you're the woman who leans out of the window and calls down: "Hey! You're running the wrong way!"

Thanks for all of your professional editing advice and for encouraging me to make it as good as I could get it before moving on.

Finally, thank you, to you, for giving this story a chance. If you liked this, you'll find more at http://deanclaytonedwards.com.

Also by Dean Clayton Edwards

<u>The Hollow Places</u> - A Novel
A journey of rescue, revenge and redemption.

Simon delivers live bodies to a psychic creature in the water. He has a natural ability for the work and is even beginning to think he might enjoy it, until the creature asks for the life of his sister, giving him a window of fewer than 24 hours to save both their lives.

Connect with Dean Clayton Edwards

Thanks very much for reading The Chair.

Next time you stand up at your computer:

- Find me on Twitter
  http://twitter.com/deancedwards

- Add me to your network on Facebook
  http://www.facebook.com/deanclaytonedwards/

- Check out what's new at my website
  http://deanclaytonedwards.com

Excerpt from The Hollow Places

Chapter One

For the driver, only three things existed: the road, the wheel and the woman in the back seat.

A glance in the mirror showed him nothing but the rear windscreen, so he took a look over his shoulder and saw that the woman hadn't moved, sitting with her head between her knees, a fall of dyed blonde hair, making burping sounds and sniffling.

"It's okay," Simon said and kept the car sliding through the darkness. He was enjoying a heightened state of awareness and sensed each turn before it appeared. His foot on the accelerator, he knew that they were unlikely to encounter anyone else on this road. It was just him and her.

When she sat up, her large, brown eyes were very dark and ringed with red. Her skin was waxy, streaked black with mascara.

"Oh-my-God, I am sorry," she sniffed and wiped her mouth with the back of her hand.

"It's okay," Simon said again.

It wasn't his car.

Unknown to her, Simon watched her wipe her hand on the fabric of the back seat and then strain to see past her ghostly reflection in the glass. He offered her a bottle of water.

"I don't think it is good for me," she said, her Parisian accent coming through. "It will just make me more ..." She gestured throwing up and had to suppress another wave of nausea. "We are nearly there?"

"This way will avoid the traffic," Simon said.

This way would avoid everyone.

Trees linked arms overhead, attempting to seal out the moonlight. Their leaves glowed preternaturally in the headlights before becoming ash-black and then scarlet as they rolled by. Ahead, a steep incline began winding down to the sea coast, but they would turn off before they reached the bottom.

"This might help," he said, winding his window part-way down.

The sound of waves smothering rocks and then sliding back, crashing and retreating, accompanied the fluttering of owls or bats and the scampering of unseen things in the trees.

He might have found it disturbing, but he was on a high now and found himself observing the fine, curly hairs on the backs of his hands before remembering the road. The road appeared to be undulating beneath him, as if their destination was sliding towards them and the car was still.

"So, you really think it is broked?" she asked, holding up her hand, which was very small and pale, except for her little finger, which was swollen and almost black.

"We need a medical opinion," Simon told her. "I'm a taxi driver."

He glanced in the mirror to see if she knew she was in trouble yet.

She was peering though the passenger windows, first

The Chair

one side and then the other. Both views offered her something that evidently upset her.

"This isn't London," she said. "Where is the hospital?

Part of him wanted her to know what was coming, because he didn't want to lie to her anymore, but he knew that lying was for the best. If their roles had been reversed, he wouldn't want to know what was coming either.

"Not far now," he said, though his heart wasn't in it.

She was starting to panic.

"Doesn't your finger hurt?" Simon asked.

"Yes," she said. "It hurts. But I can't do anything about it, so why complain?"

"Good for you," he said.

"How long you have been a taxi driver?" she asked.

"Six years," he said.

"Why six years?" she demanded to know. "Why didn't you say five or seven? It's a lie, right?"

"I always say six years," Simon admitted. "I've been saying six years for two years."

"My mother owns a boutique and my father is a designer. They have money. A lot of money."

Some people attempted to develop a rapport with him to dissuade him from murdering or raping them. This young woman had gone straight to bargaining. She was sobering up fast and in other circumstances he might have liked her, though it was a long time since he had thought of anyone but him and his sister. Their survival came first.

The turn was coming up.

The usual sensation occurred as he slowed the car. He could feel the turn 'glowing', calling to him. It was like being pulled in by tractor beam.

He flicked off the lights.

"What are you doing?" She sat forward and he got a waft of vomit and perfume.

"Sit back," he ordered her. "A rabbit in the road, that's all. Headlights dazzle them."

She flopped back in her seat and Simon completed the narrow turning into the woods.

His eyes flicked back and forth from the forest to the rear view mirror.

She was trying the doors. Of course they were locked centrally. From the look in her eyes, she appeared to be thinking about screaming, but probably didn't want to admit that she was in that much danger yet. She saw no point in accelerating events when she may still be able to talk her way out of this, whatever this was.

She sucked in a lungful of air, stifling another wave of nausea. Still and tense, she stared at her reflection in the black glass, until she was over the worst of it.

"So ... Vincent," she began. "Why don't I call my parents, before my friends do, and organise some money? Then you let me to go. It is easy to do."

"I'll do a deal with you," Simon said. "You can ask me five questions and I promise to tell you the truth, answering yes or answering no. But then you have to stop talking."

His night vision had become very good over the last few years, so he was able to discern a route ahead by squinting through the windscreen. After a few moments, however, he found that he knew when to jog left and jog right, and gradually let go of control, guided. The vehicle bounced down a new incline, crunching dirt and dead leaves. They could have been driving in a bubble at the bottom of the ocean, or bumping along over the dark side of the moon.

The Chair

"Where are you taking me?"

"Have you never played Twenty Questions? You can still have five."

"Stop fucking around," she said. "What are you doing?"

"I'm not fucking around," he said. "Four."

"Can I please go home? Please."

"No."

"Please?"

Simon stopped the car, shut off the engine and faced her. "You can ask two more questions," he told her.

Her voice thinned. "Please don't hurt me. Vincent? Are you going to ...?"

"No," Simon said.

She couldn't announce her fears out loud. She still didn't want to make it real.

Simon opened her door from the outside and held open a plastic, supermarket bag.

"Empty your pockets into this," he said.

"I don't have money," she said. "I said to you. My parents have the money."

She squirmed around on the back seat, reaching into the pockets of her skin-tight jeans. It took some time, because she only had use of her right hand. She managed to retrieve a plastic lighter, some tissues and a phone number written in blue ink on a strip of paper. She dropped each one into the bag.

"My purse is in my handbag," she said.

"Drop it in," he told her and she unzipped it, searching for the purse. "No," Simon said. "Your handbag. The whole thing."

She dropped it into the carrier and looked up into his

face, holding his gaze. He imagined how he must look to her. It was difficult, because since he had got out of the car he felt very little. He watched her face for some clue as to how he might appear to her.

After thirty seconds or so, her eyes began to tremble. Whatever she'd been searching for in his eyes, she hadn't found it.

"Time to go," he said.

She managed to punch him in the face as he leaned in, but her fist glanced off his cheek and soon he was hauling her out into the night. As she struggled, she reignited the pain in her dislocated finger and cried out, so Simon clamped one hand over her mouth and that's where it stayed as he pulled her away from the car and forced her deeper into the forest. He held her body tight against him, knowing that her attempts to scream for help would give way to sobs. Soon, he could feel her tears and snot running over his fingers, the chill in the wind making his wet hand feel icy.

When her legs gave way, he responded by picking up his pace, dragging her towards the sound of waves until they came to a clearing, where he remembered to pop her finger back into place. He muffled her howl and subsequent whimpers. A couple of minutes later, she settled and he relaxed his hold on her.

She took in her surroundings, realising that all the while they had been approaching the edge of a cliff.

"Are you going to let me go now?" she asked quietly.

It had helped him to think of it as a game, but now she was all out of questions and he was out of time.

"Yes and no," Simon said. "You're going to be okay. After a few minutes, you won't know what's happening. You won't feel anything."

The Chair

Stifling her protests, he dragged her through the rest of the clearing, towards the edge. Her eyes rolled and she stamped her bare heels, grinding her toes into the dirt, but he was much too strong for her. She was punching and kicking, but he lifted her from the ground, dumped her onto one shoulder and stood facing the drop.

Silvery clouds shrouded the moon in the dark, blue sky, and the black sea rolled below, toiling and growling up at them.

He imagined himself carrying her back to the car, setting her in the back seat, and driving back to the road before dumping her somewhere, alive, but the idea alone was enough to promote a headache. It was as if a finger penetrated the back of his skull and a sharp fingernail began peeling back a layer of brain.

"Okay!" he thought in response and winced. "I'm doing it!"

He pitched her over the edge, almost losing his footing in the process, making his stomach lurch.

She didn't scream. The last sound she made was a gasp. Perhaps she was surprised that he'd really dropped her, or perhaps she was sucking in the air for a scream that didn't have time to materialise.

Simon peered over the edge in time to see her body disappear into an enormous wave. It arced over the rocks and plucked her out of the air. Sea water crashed against the cliff, showering Simon's face, shoulders and chest. The woman's body was gone. Taken.

Only once had he been this close to the Creature.

Printed in Great Britain
by Amazon